layout: Elise Revéret

thanks to:
Valéria Sarmiento, Alban Barré

Edité avec le concours du Ministère Français chargé de la Culture - Centre National du Livre (aide à la traduction).

This translation was published with the aid of the Ministère Français chargé de la Culture - Centre National du Livre.

1 cité Riverin
F - 75010 Paris

http://www.disvoir.com

EAN 978 2 914 563 41 3

PRINTED IN EUROPE

RAOUL RUIZ

IN PURSUIT OF TREASURE ISLAND

Translated from French by

Paul Buck & Catherine Petit

PART ONE

CHAPTER I

I come from Portugal, but I have not spoken Portuguese in years. I am proud of this, even though I have never learnt to speak another language properly. I suppose you could say that makes me feel twice as Portuguese. To tell you the truth, I do have some French, but I think I must have lost my tongue in Spain and I'm reduced to asking my companion, *La Française* (she is from Barcelona), to translate these, my vernacular memoirs, now that *The Pelican* has been forced to close. And it's perhaps thanks to the rainy season, which I haven't seen like this in ages, that some details of the story, swamped by the most striking adventures (if I dare say so) are rising to the surface like the bodies of the drowned from the days of old. What a phrase that is! 'Days of old.' The words come to mind precisely at the moment I write them. I hear *La Française* calling me. Seated at a table at the back of the café in the glare of a paraffin lamp, I see her, an exercise book open before her and a pencil in her hand, as she waits poised to transcribe my multilingual memoirs into French. I listen to the thunder and to my children running around the courtyard, yelling. I close my eyes, I can feel the rain coming. I settle deep into my hammock and conjure up images of those days of old. And as I say those words aloud, past and present fade away and the booming sound of the stranger's voice resonates in my head.

"Days of old," I hear again. And I catch myself saying:

"*En los nidos de antaño, no hay pájaros hagano.*"

A fist comes crashing down on the table in the bar and the stranger utters:

"The days of old are upon us, sir."

"*The name is Coutinho.*"

I'm sure of it, my father and the visitor were speaking English, the language my mother had forbidden. Outside, it was pitch black. They sat deep in conversation, drinking brandy at the back of the bar. I don't think I had ever seen my father drunk before. I don't think I've ever seen him drunk again, either.

"Come over here, son," he said. Then, to the stranger: "This is my son."

"I see," said the stranger. "Did you sleep well, child?"

"Oh, he falls asleep anywhere," my father replied on my behalf, "except in his bed."

"Excellent," said our guest. "All great men fall off at the drop of a hat, isn't that right, Madam?"

This latter remark was directed at my mother. I hadn't noticed she was in the room till then. That was odd in itself. Why didn't she say something? I was sure she'd make a fuss, that was her way to gain attention, for she particularly detested the English language. I watched my father carefully. This was incredible! He never ignored her like this, he wouldn't dare! What the hell was going on? There he was, the most cowardly of men, chattering away with a stranger and in English to boot!

And my mother stood by, not saying anything. Suddenly, I realized why. My mother was petrified. She literally couldn't move. For there, on the table, was something extraordinary: a pile of money. I couldn't tell you how much. Two, three thousand dollars perhaps. All I can say is that I remember the floor was covered in dollars and our cat – a cat with no name – was toying with them.

Then a strong gust of wind blew through the house and we were swallowed in darkness. I sensed that my mother was going to the kitchen to fetch some matches. But before she could come back, our guest had set fire to a five dollar note and gone off in search of the toilet.

"Whose is it?" my mother whispered, referring to the money.

"Ours," my father replied. He didn't seem particularly interested.

For a few moments we heard the stranger singing, then he returned. He was a completely different person now. He was pale, and smiling. And sober. Sober as a judge.

"Yes," he said, "the olden days are now."

Then he turned to my mother and said: "Congratulations," before switching into French to express his distress:

"*Quel dommage, Madame, quel dommage*."

That night, I couldn't sleep. The stranger was pacing up and down in his room. He was restless, talking to himself out loud, accusing himself of all sorts of things. That's how I first came to hear about 'the Eye' and 'the Eagle'. What Eye? Whose Eye? Could it be a friend's, I wondered, someone who had betrayed him, a social acquaintance? And what was the Eagle? It sounded like some kind of organization, some kind of gang. Much later on, of course, I realized the Eye and the Eagle were one and the same thing, one and the same person.

But for the time being I couldn't make head or tail of the stranger's soliloquy as it droned on for two or perhaps three hours that night. Sometimes, he'd stop and break into song. Then he'd hit something and start shouting. It sounded like he was killing time, literally.

But I have a painful confession to make. It concerns my mother. In fact, it concerns my mother and the stranger. For she was there, in the room, with him. She was asking questions, she wanted to know where the money came from. And not just the money, she wanted to know about everything else as well. Of course, I couldn't miss this. I was determined to see and hear it all. I knew I'd be able to, if only I could get into the attic. With a bit of luck, I might get up the stairs without making any noise. Then I'd *see*, for sure. The Eye of God would tell me everything I wanted to know. I mustn't forget to tell you about the Eye of God. It's the only thing I still believe in, the one idea I haven't given up on. It is, in a way, my creed. This is how it goes: wherever in the world there's something happening, wherever you find your destiny taking shape, there is always a hole, a vantage-point, from which you can discover, or see, everything you need to know, in good time. And I do mean 'in good time'.

I climbed the stairs, wishing I hadn't given every step a name: Peter, Paula, Andrew, Mary. Boy, girl, boy, girl. I had developed a system according to which each stair was worth a certain number of points: three, five, ten or eight. Twenty-two steps was worth an eternity, cost a lifetime. They were singing now. They had woken my father up. He had joined them in the room. He was setting fire not to a banknote, but to a notebook. I recognized it straightaway. That book was the hotel's accounts! My father, the most cautious bookkeeper in the world, was setting his books alight. He burnt the lot. And then I was granted the grand finale. My God, I'll never forget it! What chaos! But I couldn't tear myself away, painful though it was, and such a confusing spectacle. As it turned out, my father's imminent death was to spare us many useless explanations. But what about me? Time and time again, since those days, the Eye of God has provided me with a key to the future. I have often been able to foresee my own adventures. This is my tale. I tell it for my children. Here, in this remote, lost corner of the Ecuadorian jungle, I want my children to know the real story of their father's life.

I mustn't make up stories. After all, there is a moral to this one.

But there is just one thing I must say: everything somehow fell into place that night and I learnt more then than during the whole of the rest of my life. Anyway, this is what I saw through the Eye of God: a single book with a lot of odd-looking objects scattered around it, objects which, on closer inspection, turned out to be a collection of small marbles, or, rather, glass eyes. One of them, in fact, was the eye the stranger had referred to in his long soliloquy. I could see the book in the middle of the floor and around it, thrown like dice, a good dozen eyes, all staring up at me.

The next day, when I got up, my parents were still fast asleep, so it was for me to open up. We were waiting for a coach load of tourists, Germans this time. They were due to arrive about midday. It was pouring with rain (as usual in these parts), and freezing cold. Who would have thought so, in the tropics! By a scientific process of elimination, I managed to find the best hiding-place from which to eavesdrop on the tourists' complaints.

"Oh God," they whined, "look how it rains in the tropics!"

"Oh no, it's even snowing!" someone else uttered in dismay.

Well, what do you expect? I thought. Of course we always

ended up feeling sorry for those poor refugees coming from the North, confronted by our winters.

"Yes, Madam," we would commiserate, "it's a terrible shame it gets so cold in the tropics. It's hard to get used to tropical snow!"

You have to understand being sarcastic was about the only fun we had in those days. But let's get back to the tourists of that day. We only had three servants in the hotel and they were doing their best – none too convincingly I have to say – to look as if they were overworked. Around eleven, my mother appeared. She was superb, graciously condescending to everyone. She showed no sign of surprise at my presence, although under normal circumstances she would have felt obliged to ask why I wasn't at school, more as a matter of conscience than out of any real concern that I should be properly educated. I suppose she had given up hope.

She knew I would never go back to school after what I had witnessed the previous night.

As it turned out, we coped with the coach load very well. I took them down to the caves, then I showed them the old fishing harbour and the road that led nowhere. I knew my part, I knew how much they'd enjoy it, providing they were reasonably well-educated people, which they were, for the most part. Invariably, in every party, there was someone who would take me under their wing: a nice old lady or some newly-weds. On this occasion, an old gentleman took a particular shine to me. The others seemed to treat him with a great deal of consideration, but it took me a long time to realize why. He was blind. He had a curious habit of deliberately falling behind the rest of the group. Ostensibly, something on the horizon seemed to catch his attention and he would do his best to look preoccupied. Inevitably, we lost him. The leader started to panic.

"Blind men," he informed us, "are bad luck."

He knew, he added, because his father had been blind and look what happened to him. Night fell and still there was no sign of the blind man. God, what a palaver! First they wanted torches for a search party, then they wanted us to call the police. Here, there and everywhere, they ordered us.

"Hold on, we're not in your country!"

There was nothing my father could do to calm them down.

"Be a bit more patient, please."

My father, it must be said, was in his element. He was enjoying being at the centre of other people's problems. A blind man lost without trace. Ten times, at least, he rang the police. He sent a car to pick up the fishermen. But what did I care? At last, here was some action. They could call in firemen, they could call in the army for all I cared. None of them knew the coast as well as I did. Not one knew the forbidden zones like I did. I knew them like the back of my hand. I knew the caves where ghostly voices *sang*. Eventually, everyone had to be fed. You could have heard a pin drop at the tables. They were desperately trying to fathom the eerie whistling sound. What did it mean? The *companions* (as I called the voices in the caves) excelled themselves that night and their disembodied serenade mingled strangely with the wailing of the fishermen's wives.

The police, I forgot to say, arrived just before dinner. They talked with my father for a long time.

"Has someone got a photograph of the blind man?" they asked.

Now everyone followed my example in calling him the blind man. But I was playing a waiting game. I decided to go up to my room. I was tired and, for once, I felt like sleeping in my own bed.

I don't know at what time I was awoken by a cold draught. Someone had opened my window.

"You are no longer tired, are you child? You'd sleep much better at night if you didn't drop off during the day. You never sleep properly at night, do you?"

This was the stranger, smoking his pipe in my room. He stared out of the window towards the beach.

"They're still looking for him," he said. "What do you reckon has happened to our blind friend then?"

"Your blind friend?" I couldn't help querying.

He laughed.

"Don't jump to conclusions."

He got to his feet.

"Do you know what? I think you should get a good night's sleep, just for once. Have you ever *really* had a good night's sleep?"

His handkerchief was smothering my face before I had time to react. I thought I saw a glass eye drop from his pocket. I made a last effort to fight him off, but my dreams were racing off towards the shore.

It took me a good while to realize that the scream I heard, that sounded more like the petrified shrieking of a hysterical old English lady, was in fact my father's laughter. He was laughing and laughing, quite out of control. The tourists had gone. In one corner of the bar, the stranger stood drinking. I knew they were watching me, the stranger and my mother. Somehow they seemed to be communicating with each other through me. I am used to chloroform now, but at the time it made my head thick and woolly. I had trouble walking. I felt my way down the stairs, one foot at a time. The steps creaked, as usual, except that now the whole world seemed to be creaking.

"They've found him."

My father was off again. This time he was laughing for real, overdoing it a bit.

"Just shut up, old man," said the stranger.

"Why should I?" said my father. "Go on, why should I?"

"Come on," said my mother, wiping away the traces of blood.

Though my father wore a bandage, he was bleeding and waving his arms around wildly in the air. And laughing, he just couldn't stop laughing...

"You be quiet, or I'll do it again."

"For pity's sake," my mother begged, "not in front of the child."

"I wouldn't worry about that," the stranger muttered.

"Go away," said my mother, acknowledging my presence.

"No," said my father. "He's got to stay. He must stay because it's all going to come down on him one day, isn't it? He's the last in line. What's the good in hiding the truth."

"Truth!" said the stranger. "What truth? There's no such thing in this story."

"Oh, really," said my father. "I thought we were in the presence of truth. I thought truth was blind, like justice."

The stranger hit my father, hard. I turned and ran. I ran and ran, for a long time. I only stopped when I reached the beach. The fishermen were still there with their flaming torches. They might as well make themselves useful I thought.

I recognized Vasco among them. He was leaning over the water, shining an electrical torch into the waves, attracting the fish.

"Here," he said. "Want some?"

He showed me the best crab in his basket.

He pretended not to notice my tears.

"What a business, eh?" he sighed. "He's dead, isn't he? That's the way it goes. He's probably better off that way, poor bloke. Can you imagine not being able to see anything at all? It must be really awful. Still, that's life."

"Have they found him?"

"The blind man? I guess so."

"But..."

"Well, they've found his jacket, his papers and all that. But not his body. It's got to be suicide..."

My mother was calling me, but I didn't want to know. I left. I had a good spot, down there, in Polyphemus' Throat. I could still hear my mother calling. She was looking for me, she sounded worried. Then my father joined in. And the stranger too. But I was already far away, safe, deep inside the cave... Polyphemus was singing. And I went back to sleep. It was the silence of the waking day that awoke me. I knew it was going to be a fine day. The weather was always good when the *companions* sang their serenade in the cave. I was shivering and hungry. But I was pleased the tourists would not be there today and I was pleased it was going to be a fine day. I was about to start singing the song of the *companions* when a voice interrupted. It was a male voice, talking about the eyes, of course, and a book. I almost screamed when I saw him. It was my father. He was bleeding profusely, stumbling over the rocks. My cry remained frozen in my throat and a deadly silence fell in Polyphemus' belly. The sun rose across the sea, and the silence slaughtered us, my father and I. But what on earth was he doing there in his Sunday best, the suit he was married in? There was something funny about him, something not quite right. This wasn't my father's natural walk. Something dropped from his pocket. He turned round sharply. It was the blind man, dressed in my father's clothes. Suddenly, I felt ashamed, and a wave of hatred came over me. The blind man was alive. My father must have saved him. They had simulated the suicide. It was all an act, a pretence. This was preposterous. Why didn't I want to speak to him? Why did my instincts warn me against going up to him to say how happy I was he was alive? Why wasn't I going to help him escape?

With unprecedented agility, he left the cave and vanished from sight.

It started to rain softly. I looked up at a blue sky and listened to the *companions* singing. I followed the blind man up the road, towards the volcanoes. Now I wanted to stop him. But everything that happened was pre-ordained, as if already written in the book.

"Enough", he said. "Where am I?"

"They're all looking for you," I replied. "You're on the radio. Everyone thinks you're dead."

"And how is it I'm not?"

There was something odd about the way he spoke. He was mimicking my father's Portuguese accent, exaggerating it shamelessly in the same way as my father.

"Alright, my child," he said. "I think we'd better have a word. That's why they sent you, isn't it? They're using you, you know, because it's easier to communicate through children. Grown ups can't talk directly to each other, isn't that right? Here, come here. You are my only... what shall I say?... the only friend I've got. That's right, eh? We're friends. You are my only hope. Are you there?"

"Yes," I said flatly. I wasn't giving an inch.

"Come closer then. Come on. I won't hurt you."

I could see by the expression on his face that he wanted to grab hold of my arm and twist it. I knew he wanted to hurt me. The whole thing was too stupid.

"Here, lad," the blind man insisted.

Then I did something I never thought I'd have the guts to do. I threw a stone at him. Then another, before he had time to recover. And another. And more... I can't recall everything that happened after that. He was yelling in pain. I knew this would work. I knew this would get them all off my back. The blind man knew that too.

"Alright," he said. "You've won. You and your allies. We'll see, we'll see what happens now. One day, you'll understand."

"There's nothing to understand," I said.

It was hot. The sun was burning our faces. The blind man and I, both stared in the same direction. At least, that's how I look at it now. Immutable, fixed forever, in torrid sunshine. Fixed and eternal. On the wall a marble plaque read: "Here lived R.L.Stevenson, the immortal author of *Voyage to Madeira*, 1872-73."

CHAPTER II

Several days passed before my mother and I could speak together. As for my father, he had decided not to step out of his room any longer. He just said he wasn't at home. Poor man! He had never really made his presence in the hotel felt as much as he did during those few days. He called for my mother, then beat her. They told me he wasn't eating. The stranger had suddenly left for the mainland, but people saw him in Funchal. Oh, he was there alright. He was watching out for us.

Can you imagine what life is like for a twelve year-old boy suddenly turned into a grand inquisitor? I will tell you. He is constantly asking questions and, though people reply, he still feels totally isolated. He is restless and uneasy in his own home, so he goes for long walks. He is, in fact, terribly bored. He doesn't know what to do except drift, soullessly, through the endless stream of days.

Sundays are the worst: a day that never ends, a day that is always the same. If I had known my whole life was going to be dogged by this endless boredom, I would have given the whole thing up.

Well, I suppose I already had, in a way. But I wasn't exactly alone. I had my friends in the village, they filled my dreams. They at least said they sympathized.

Then one day the stranger returned. There was something different about him. He wore a beard now. He never stopped smiling. He came back to us one splendid winter day and stayed forever. Three days later, my father was cured. He started smiling and laughing too. The three of them became inseparable. Gradually, the stranger took over the running of the hotel. He never slept. His head was always full of figures and numbers, like some kind of Kabbalist.

On stormy nights, he would read out loud. Yes, and sing. He'd sing his readings. Until the day of the parrots. How on earth did those parrots end up at our place? Later on I found out they were part of a scheme to make the hotel a bit more attractive, to give it an exotic touch for the tourists. They thought they ought to capitalize on the name of our street as well, so they decided to change its name to *Ballantrae.*

My father faded away, gently. He rarely left his room. As for my mother, she quickly subsided into a kind of mild pettiness. She spent her time imagining minor incidents of theft where they could not possibly have taken place. At least, that was her pretence, which greatly pleased my dying father.

Meanwhile, bloodstains appeared on the stairs and the walls of all the bedrooms. Of course, they were washed off as soon as they were discovered. However, there did seem to be some kind of conspiracy afoot. In the end we grew more and more accustomed to the shapes of these bloodstains. People read into them what they wished, including signs of the future. We had fewer and fewer customers, which was hardly surprising.

In July, I fell ill. A fever took hold of me as I was wiping one of the more persistent stains from the wall. I thought I saw the shape of the blind man's face, as if he had returned to haunt me because of my refusal to have anything to do with him. I felt the weight of the stone in the hand that I was about to throw at him. Then I had the feeling of climbing right up, all alone.

Finally I started hearing my father's laughter, that hysterical womanish giggle. Several nights running I imagined him shrieking with convulsive laughter. I saw the blood, but I heard the bloodstains. They were dancing, supple, crackling, generous in their swelling slopes.

The colour of night, however, remained the same. An overwhelming blue, which nevertheless brought me some form of solace.

Let me resume.

I said the stranger returned. He did nothing all morning, barely dragged himself around in the afternoon, and slept all night. However, in the evening he took a taxi into Funchal. He was gambling. It seemed he often won. And sometimes, he'd take my mother along.

Do muscles have a memory of their own? Of course, the fact that my knee hurts so badly obscures a shameful memory I should like to suppress, but that is the point: the scene retreats into the background and I have something else to talk about. Like here and now, for instance. My knee is in agony. Ouch! That staircase, that triumphal march up the stairs. I wasn't sleeping at night. I was convinced I was losing blood. Every night as I watched the moon wax into fullness at my window and saw it carve the shadows of my lead soldiers (wearing the uniform of Napoleon's Italian campaign) into sharp, neat silhouettes, I was sure I had lost a little more blood. That night I know I was not asleep but still the sound of the drums and the marching must have been a dream. And I know the agony of my knee commanded the comings and goings.

The beating. I should have expected it would happen in that darkness. Why turn on the light? The blind have no use for light. But what about the other one? There were two of them. They came straight for me. What hunger! What dizziness! They punched me right in the stomach. I knew I would never be the same person again. The pain isn't hard to take, that comes later. No, it's knowing what's about to happen just before it does which is difficult to swallow, since swallowing is what it's all about. They hit hard, hard and fast. Methodically. They beat me methodically. And the marching didn't stop, because the others arrived. By others, I mean my father, my mother and the stranger. The others arrived, armed with the most frightening passivity. (Now the pain has a different meaning: the agony of raw shame. I was ashamed.)

"Is that it?" enquired the stranger. He alone had the power to halt everything. "Are you satisfied?"

"He deserved it," my father remarked helpfully as my mother looked on, her mind elsewhere. Her fingers betrayed her real preoccupation, she was counting something as she watched, doing calculations.

"Right," said the blind man, "that's us quits, child. As for you," he said, turning to the stranger, "I'm sure you'll do me the honour of accepting this humble gift."

He pulled out a black handkerchief and said: “Take it.”

“Oh, that!” said the stranger.

But he had gone quite white. He knew that we knew. Worse, he knew that our suspicions would, in the end, take him away, far away from us. Suspicions. That’s all it was. No one had any proof.

A tom-tom beat of swelling bruises gradually replaced the thud of marching steps in my brain. The hotel fell into silence. How many hearts beat in my body? My knees, my belly and my jaw were all alive with painful rhythm.

“Poker?” the stranger suggested.

The two men had withdrawn when my mother began her litany.

“My son, I want you to know that everything that happens is only destiny. But it will be alright. Don’t be afraid. They know what they’re doing. They knocked you about a bit, but they haven’t really hurt you, have they? Tomorrow, it will all be forgotten. You see, men are like children. It’s all very simple. The fact is that, years ago, your father got himself into a bit of trouble. Nothing outside the law, you know, but the problem is times change and people’s idea of what’s wrong and what’s legal changes too. Your father is an honourable man. He’s been a good father to you. He’s just a little upset at the moment. All this has got to him. Do you understand? Old stories he’d almost forgotten have come back to haunt him. He didn’t even remember these people existed. He’s just a little shaken, that’s all, like you are. Just remember, this is nothing to worry about. Sleep tight, darling. Kiss kiss.”

They were laughing downstairs. “Just like the good old days,” someone said. They prevented me from sleeping. Then I felt something. One thing, that’s right. Nothing more. I shuddered, like shivering in a cold shower. I was scared. Fear had overtaken pain. Now fear was ahead of the game. From now on, everything I did, I did out of fear. Why, for instance, was the stranger going up to his room all by himself? I knew he wasn’t tired. If there was one thing I was sure of, it was the music of our house. And I could tell the stranger wasn’t tired from the sound of his footsteps on the stairs. I had to go up, make sure I saw it all happen. I was perfect. Nobody would have heard a thing. To this day, no one knew I was there, watching everything through the Eye of God.

The stranger took out his revolver. He cleaned it as carefully as he could. Then he went out. Far away, the shots woke me.

Then a voice:

"The boy! Where's the boy?!"

I knew I'd never have time to get back to my room.

"Gone".

"I thought you said you'd given him some pills."

"Calm down!"

"The stupid bitch! The whore! Where the hell is he?"

They ran up and down the stairs looking for me. Then, silence. My mother started crying. Downstairs, the stranger entered his room. He paced up and down, stopped, then started again. For a while he read a book. I was dead tired, but I couldn't fall asleep. That's when the noise started, a horrible rumbling sound in my guts. I was starving. I was choking with hunger and pain. I wanted to cry. How could I stifle the rumbling?

That was it. The stranger stopped reading. He looked around him. Then, cautiously, he lifted his eyes. He was staring in my direction. He was staring beyond me, beyond the Eye of God. Was he smiling already? Yes and no. The situation was too serious, I can't remember the specific physical aspects. He removed his revolver and took aim at the Eye.

Then he fired. The bullet went through the ceiling and, at last, I was able to sleep. The memory of those extraordinary nights is still alive to this day. What explanation did they give? Did they manage to hush it all up? The thought of Sundays upon Sundays, stretching into an infinite future, confined by these four stone walls and pelted by the eyes of people who dare not look you in the eye. I come from a land where people look without seeing. The price they pay is high: they build themselves a frozen labyrinth whose viscosity marks you forever.

What was at stake here? At home, at least, everyone must have known what was happening. Particularly since I then had to undergo a process of several weeks of simulated mourning. Has nobody ever killed you? It's quite an experience, I assure you. I discovered it the following day, in the way my mother avoided looking at me, in my father's obscene and quite uncontrollable delight and in the way the stranger insisted on fixing me with his *eyeball* stare. Oh, I almost forgot. From then on he was to be known as 'the Captain'. From then on Captain it would be. But, of course, I should really have begun with the funeral. What happened is this. The cat with no name woke me and then jumped out the window, disappearing off towards the beach. Down there I saw mum and dad silhouetted, looking rather like my lead soldiers in the moonlight as, half-asleep, they performed the rites of mother nature. Acting on the Captain's orders, they were burying the corpses of my two tormentors.

But let's return to the cat. Its final hours had probably rocked my death-like sleep. After the gun went off, I checked my eyes were okay. There were three of them. There had been three shots. And the last shot, I am convinced, hit the cat. I glanced around the room. No one had thought to look for me up here. It was perfect. The cat was looking at the window, it was breathing with difficulty. It was dying, but dying with dignity. A model of resignation. I tried to stroke it but this proved to be a fatal mistake. It scratched me viciously and in so doing recovered its fear. It started running around in circles. That was a shame, because a few seconds earlier it really had been quite a classic sight. Human ineptitude contaminates everything man comes into contact with. I was treated to the whole number. The beast tried to claw its insides out, twisting and turning and writhing all over the place in its pathetic attempt to combat pain. I tried to throw it through the window, but, with a final bout of effort, the cat managed to jump of its own accord and vanished.

So there I was at the window, dominating the scene from above. As usual, my father applied himself to the dirty job. I watched him shovel pile after pile of black sand from the grave, plunging meticulously deep into the recesses of his own sad, inner world. Eventually, he spoke. To himself, naturally. But it was enough to set the others off. My mother started piling one veiled reproach after another on him. She seemed to have retrieved some slight, long-forgotten shreds of feminine charm. Meanwhile, the Captain played, as usual, the provocative foil to this marital scene, managing to seem at once humble, in the rolling of a cigarette, and wise, in his inspection of the dead. Yes, my father had been given the privilege of the offended. And they were definitely there, the blind man and the other. We're not counting our misinterpretation. If I dare say so, the blind man had seen it all. He alone was honour bound for the scene, a pretty mask of unadulterated monstrosity; and his henchman, the thought of him still makes me laugh, whom they buried standing to attention. He must have been a schoolteacher, the henchman, a man whose entire vision of the world was encompassed in the patriotic fluttering of a flag. The most astonishing feature of this whole little spectacle and, if I may say so, the most disgusting thing about it, was the total absence of anything resembling blood. Not a drop. Well, perhaps that's an exaggeration, but there can't have been very much; come to think of it, I am positive there wasn't a single drop, which made my own little kingdom, with its three wise eyes bathed in a pool of iridescent blood, seem quite unnecessarily dramatic: a non-existent and stinking vantage-point. Down there those riddled corpses seemed miserly indeed by comparison. As though they had somatised the spirit of the mouth shut tight.

I have said they were talking, but actually it was more like three soliloquies that, from time to time, accidentally converged to form a dialogue. Oh, they were paying for having turned a blind eye now, weren't they? Turning your nose up was very hurtful, wasn't it? What a nice little performance! You've guessed, I was angry. Well, why not? Why shouldn't I?

Finally my father emerged from the pit. They dumped both corpses in a heap at the bottom and recovered it with the turf. The whole thing was over in a jiffy. I expected them to snuggle up together for a quick nap, best of pals and all that, any second now, but no, there must have been a lot more business to attend to because they disappeared into my father's office and sat deep in conversation till midday. The calculator was having a field day.

CHAPTER III

Night surrounded me. I realized it must have been about six in the morning. Today was Tuesday, a day of sacrifice. There was smoke all over the island. I escaped to the mountains. I was certain nobody had seen me. I stopped once, just once, to take a good, long look around. The vet's van almost ran me over. A thought suddenly occurred to me: I imagined each of my thighs was a cat dying, crawling with ants. But my thighs weren't dead. They clawed around in a vacuum, playing games with the white ball joints of the kneecaps. This expedition was a right mess. I had to act now, or hide, and I certainly wasn't about to be scared away by a dead cow barely out of its milky grave. I can't remember what happened next. Dawn had not yet broken over the slaughterhouses but the island was already aflame. Someone recognized me. I didn't respond to his friendly wave: I didn't trust it, I just ran off. Why did I feel so guilty?

I slept in the open throughout the morning.

The island was on fire, alright: the heat, the flames, the stench of burnt flesh. I woke up hungry. If I kept on walking in a straight line towards the snow-capped mountain, I knew I took the risk of meeting up with some friends who often went there for picnics. But nothing. I must have strayed off the path at some point, I was lost. That was my fault. I'd never really had any desire to explore the island and now I realized I was going round and round in circles.

I came across a few stray groups of tourists. Now that I think of it, I clearly recall this whole episode as happening at night: icy moon, the kind of bluish dark worth dying for, and, everywhere, the island crawling with ants, just like my legs. All the roads to Funchal were jammed with cars and coach loads of nervous tourists, smiling like the blind. Yes, the whole scene happens at night. And in silence. I see it again, the cold moonlight piercing the snuffles of the slaughtered cattle. As I recall, the events of the next few weeks had a different feel to them. They stand distinct from my other memories, frozen as these are in expectant quietness, in a silence that bears witness against my family's secret doings.

At about nine in the evening, I went home. They were all waiting. They said they'd looked for me everywhere. People claimed to have seen me all over the island. I had suddenly become quite *popular*. I have to admit that I was relieved. Everything, I mean absolutely everything, had returned to normal. There was no trace of any kind of disquiet, not one searching look. They were putting on a show for me undoubtedly, but at least the show didn't come to an abrupt ending. I suspect I was punished for staying out late. We all sat down to eat and suddenly everyone relaxed. What an evening that was! They laughed, positively oozing friendliness and good cheer. My father sang. Yes, he sang in his high pitched voice:

Fifteen men on the dead man's chest
Yo-ho-ho, and a bottle of rum!

Well, at first, I laughed along with everybody else. I didn't know the song yet and I had no idea of the maze of references it was leading us into. How was I supposed to know it was the key to the story I'm telling you now?

The Captain took up the chorus, in English, and then my mother followed, in French. When my turn came, I stood up to sing slowly and solemnly, for I was about to enter the strange fraternity of the living dead. A weird shrill voice, a voice I didn't know, emanated from my throat. My lips were moving, but my voice was someone else's. One voice, then another and another came from me. Everyone was laughing, laughing like mad. A thousand voices sang in my head. I wanted to leave. As I opened the door, a crazed chorus of parrots burst in. There were dozens of them, all singing the pirate song. And from behind, my relatives joined in too.

I felt the Captain's hand on my head. I smelt his breath. He stared into my face. He knew. He had guessed.

"Who scratched you?" he asked.

"The cat," I said.

"What cat?"

"The cat with no name."

The Captain slapped my face. A second ground me to a halt.

"Don't you dare strike my son, not without permission."

Who would have thought it! My father coming into his own!

The Captain sighed and downed another glass. Then everything continued as before.

That night, I couldn't sleep. I heard all kinds of noises. I could see in the dark. I thought to myself, I can see because of what happened to the blind man. He has impregnated everything he touched or guessed or figured out as he stumbled around with his own sticky brand of light. I can see with the eyes of the cat with no name, I thought to myself. I shan't rest until I am gutted, like it was. Also, I thought, they know I can see in the dark, there must be an Eye of God in my room too. They're watching me, they're going to discover my clairvoyance is make-believe.

I went up to *see*. Upstairs, the Eye of God was shining, solitary amid abandoned toys and old boots piled up on top of an old sewing-machine. Downstairs, the Captain was reading in his freshly painted room.

I could tell he was waiting for something to happen. Perhaps they were waiting for me. I scarcely had time to lie down and glue my eye to one of the three holes before they rushed on stage. My mother entered and a strange conversation struck up.

"Your son knows. He's seen something."

"What does he know?"

"More than we do, that's the point. He knows more than we do."

My mother burst out laughing.

"You love accusing my son of things, don't you? Anyone would think you were jealous!"

"I bet you miss that, don't you?"

"What?"

"Jealousy."

"What a stupid idea!"

The Captain grabbed her and kissed her roughly. Then the weirdest part of the scene happened. They started dancing around in the middle of the room. It was as if they were doing it for someone to see. But the only person watching was me. I couldn't make head or tail of it.

"Alright, enough foolishness," said the Captain. "It's time we got down to business."

"The ball's in your court," said my mother.

Nothing happened. There was a long silence. Then a muffled sound of coughing.

"What! Already!" said the Captain.

"That's what I said," said my mother. "There's nothing to be afraid of, he can see everything, but he can't hear us. Get on with it."

The Captain sighed and started kissing her again.

"Right," he said. "It's time we made a move," he added, stroking her leg insistently. "He's way ahead of us. He's already in touch with the others."

"The others? I thought we'd dealt with that…"

"What? You mean the blind man? He was nothing, but he had the time to contact the Eagle, in which case we're…"

"You're right," said my mother, "we'd better act swiftly."

They were half-naked now. They were acting out the whole business in slow motion. I realized my father must be spying on them through a whole in the wall, stage right.

"But what about my husband?"

"What about your husband?"

"Well, I can't just leave him behind!"

"Why not?"

"You don't know my son. He's pitiless. He'd kill him. He'll kill you too, given a chance."

The Captain burst out laughing, a laugh that was deep and convincing.

In reality he was thoroughly enjoying himself. He tried to manoeuvre and turn his back on my father so as not to spoil the atmosphere, but that only made things too obvious.

They realized the game had lost its charm and that they'd have to take things a lot further. I closed my eyes. This whole business didn't exactly fit in with my idea of moral behaviour. But how could I be sure if I didn't watch to see what happened? And above all, how could I bear to hear what I was hearing without enduring at least a glimpse of it?

"I'm not joking, we've got to act now. I don't want to kill him, I don't like killing people. Besides, people never die for good."

And they resumed their performance. The whole house creaked in time with them. I have already mentioned the creaking music of our house that secretly accompanies my memories. Our hotel had previously served as a prison and a primary school, a convent and a post office. In its own way, the house was *communicating*. The companionship of this parallel world added a splendid ingredient to the conspiracies within its walls. This certainly applied to my expeditions up the stairs for instance, and it applied to everyone else too. To this day, my head is full of the creakings of our house, layer upon layer of creakings, thanks to which every day I spent there has an unmistakeable aural identity of its own. Sometimes, I hear something that reminds me of the peculiar, creaking music of one particular day. I recognize it, then, and distinguish it from among a thousand other, similar days, seeing everything that happened in specific detail. The sound of a match striking, of car brakes or laughter followed by a door closing. Each one of these sounds is enough, any little thing, any noise can trigger it. So, today, that unmistakeable day appears with all its dead, lit by the light of a paraffin lamp, and the thought of it brought about that storm in heat.

Downstairs, overwhelmed by its own stupidity, the show was flagging like a grass-snake in the sun. What a make-believe! Those two were conspiring for the sheer pleasure of it, and out of a perversity to display the opposite of their intentions.

"No, I know you'll never dare. There are too many of them."

"Well, let's split it in two then."

"What, darling?"

"This."

This turned out to be in a small bag that found itself conveniently placed in my line of vision through the Eye of God.

I had seen it before. No, on second thoughts, it wasn't the same as the blind man's. But it did look like a whole host of similar bags I had seen my father's friends carrying in the past.

A few months previously, a group of his old friends had come round to see him one Sunday just before Christmas. They'd brought some gifts, among which my lead soldiers (the ones representing the battalions of Napoleon's Italian campaign) and a small, wooden statue from Africa, a beautiful little piece that I ended up burying in the garden to banish certain improper thoughts from my mind. As it happened, I had chosen a spot not far from where our two corpses now lay. All must have been connected, somehow.

There had been three of them, these friends of my father's, and their wives had come along too. Three noisy ladies dressed up to look like nothing much. I deduced they were Spanish. They spent the night there. My father and his friends stayed up late playing cards and I had the impression my father lost badly. Not, I think, money but something much more precious. After that, my parents argued constantly. That game of cards became one of their favourite topics, something of a ritual, and one day I was stupid enough to ask my mother what the stake had been.

"His soul probably," she had replied with calculated indifference.

But I could tell from the way my father went white that she was not exaggerating.

So my father had lost his soul.

Or, at any rate, he had lost his wife, a fact which showed in all sorts of different, little ways. It has even become her favourite joke. "What do you call a man who gambles his wife away?"

It was only much later that I understood he had forsaken his rights. What rights? The whole thing was so imposing that it did teach me, because it seemed to matter so much and because it was kept so secret, just how pompous those people could be. There was indeed a secret, but the secret was invented *a posteriori*, to disguise the fact that money had been saved. And the money saved was itself nothing but a fiction to disguise the emptiness, an emptiness which, alone, could satisfy them now they had embarked upon this insane quest.

Well, they had not gone to the limit. On balance, the show turned out to be reasonably decent. Nevertheless, they went through the whole performance all over again with a relentlessness that, despite my tender years, I found amusing. What a lot of effort to conceal a secret that did not exist, that had not been determined as yet.

"It's a matter of killing."

Steal, kill... they were a little short on imagination: a heavy and overcooked meal. They had committed murder for the sheer fun of it and now they needed a reason for having done it. It was my job to find one.

The next scene was predictable. I should have seen it coming. My father appeared in his grey suit.

"So now one doesn't bother to knock?" asked the Captain.

"That's how it is," muttered my father, with total lack of conviction.

"Well, let's talk about it," the Captain said, opening hostilities.

"Get dressed first," said my father.

"He'll never learn bad manners, will he?" my mother interjected for good measure.

Seen from above, this domestic tiff made a strange impression.

"This is none of my business," said the Captain as he promptly walked through to the toilet, leaving the door open. I presume he wanted us all to hear, probably his idea of a joke.

As soon as my father was alone with my mother, he kissed her. Then he switched off the light. I couldn't believe my eyes. This was far more exciting than anything I would read later. They groaned and moved around. I shut my eyes. The light was back on: my father was on his knees and my mother stood above him, staring challengingly into his eyes. They had seen each other in the dark and now they defied each other blindly. Each of us had been put in our place. The Captain was laughing and I was laughing too, for all I was worth. It really was hilarious: I forgot to say they were twenty feet apart. The ice had been broken. The game restarted. All talking at once, they went off together. I heard the car start, then their laughter receding into the distance.

Then I heard another car. I went downstairs and looked through the window. Yes, there was definitely another car. Two men climbed out and came towards the hotel. Something needed to be done. I couldn't get Manuel without crossing the street and Antonia would be no good at all. I rushed upstairs, into my father's office for I knew where he kept his revolver. I heard them talking.

"What about the boy?"

"Tough luck!"

The gun was not there. It was nowhere to be seen. I went back downstairs.

All I was hoping to find was his shotgun. As I opened the kitchen door, I knocked something over and a bottle broke. The whole house creaked. They were in the living room and they knew I was near.

"Are you there, boy?"

"Don't be afraid, it's just some old friends of your dad's."

"Is he in? We knocked. Did we wake you up? Where's the light?"

At last, I found the gun. Was it loaded?

"Alright lad, we're going to turn the light on. Is that okay with you?"

I heard swearing, then one of the visitors tumbled to the ground.

"There's someone else here."

"What? Do you think the Crab has played another of his tricks?"

"Crab? Are you there? Time you came out, if you know what I mean. We've got an awful lot to talk about."

"Okay Crab, we know you mean well. Everyone knows that. We're very fond of you Crab, that's why I came in person. You know the Eagle never goes anywhere unless it really means a lot to him. But, Crab, remember this: if there's one thing the Eagle can't stand, it's wasting his time. You know that, don't you, Crab? You wouldn't want the Eagle to be wasting his time, would you, Crab?"

"Well, Crab, are we friends?"

I had the gun. I couldn't think of anything else but my gun.

"Who's there!"

The other guy was losing his nerve.

"Right then, are you coming out or what?"

Finally, they found the kitchen light. I dropped the gun. It went off of its own accord.

And there, before me, I saw... my father. That's right. That man standing there covered in blood was definitely my father. He shuddered and fell.

"Oh, my God!" said the other man. "There was no need for that. There really was no need for that." He took the body in his arms and dragged it out.

"There really was no need!" he shouted.

On the floor, in a pool of blood, lay a single, glass eye.

At that moment, I realized I was stark naked.

CHAPTER IV

Early the next morning, I packed my suitcase. The most disparate group of belongings found their way in there. At first, sensibly, I arranged shirts and socks and a jumper. But then suddenly I emptied out the whole lot and filled the whole case with all the different soaps and shampoos I could lay my hands on. I crammed the lot into the case. And books. Why not take books along too (me, who never reads)? So I emptied all the soaps and started over with books. I went through this deranged process four or five times. I couldn't honestly have told you what I ended up taking, but the sun was rising and I wanted to catch the six-thirty bus. I had to make a move. My suitcase was heavy, of course. I wondered, as I made my way to the bus, what I had finally, and illogically, brought along. What had I left behind? I had left things scattered all over the house. You see, in the end I had packed more than one suitcase. There were three on the first floor landing, I knew that, and another couple outside the door of the office. And another, I think, by the kitchen. In fact, I seem to have packed every single thing in the house, including my father's papers, bottles of fragrance, and ties, so many ties. Oh, and yes, a gun. Where was the gun? Did I have it with me, in this suitcase I was carrying, or had I left it behind?

Luckily, no one knew me on the bus. It was as if I was already elsewhere. Neither Paulo nor Antonia had seen me leave.

I took a seat at the rear of the bus. My journey began. It was like something out of a film. Within a few minutes, I had fallen asleep, and by the time I woke up, the bus was already on the outskirts of Funchal. Near me, some people were speaking English. They were discussing the notorious Crab.

"So you reckon they're going to get away with it this time," one of them was saying, "because I'm not so sure."

That voice was familiar. Apparently they hadn't noticed me. They were in good humour. In fact, they were polishing off a bottle of whisky and, clearly, it wasn't the first of the morning. I could have sworn they were not the same as my visitors of the previous night, but then how many of them could there be? I didn't dare sit up. They were just in front of me. And for the rest of the trip I kept hearing odd fragments of conversation, snatches full of familiar words, none of which made sense. It was like finding bits of a jigsaw puzzle that fitted together to make a disappointingly boring picture, something a trifle sad and vaguely unpleasant.

Of one thing, I was certain: my parents were criminals. They were crooks. Either that or they were involved in some incredibly elaborate game. Or...

They left the bus with their suitcases near the harbour. I wasn't about to let them escape (don't ask me why). They were still talking, but now they were talking about my family. My father was called the Fox and my mother, Lily.

"Dream on! You know Lily would never agree to that."

"You'll see."

"Look, she only ever wanted one thing and now she has it. He's only got to die and then... I tell you, she's done very well for herself."

"Just look at the way she walks."

"What's funny about that?"

They were having a beer down by the harbour. I sat down on my suitcase, listening to what they were saying.

"There he is!"

"About bloody time too!"

"What are you doing?"

Their boss had grabbed me by the neck.

"Hello, young man..."

"Who's that boy?"

"Has he been following you?"

"Take it easy, Eagle, take it easy."

How on earth could I have mistaken him for my father! He was smaller, but much better built, more agile. There was nothing sinister about his smile, when he did smile. On the contrary, he looked like a choir boy modestly acknowledging compliments he knows to be well-deserved.

"Alright, we'll call it a coincidence," he said. "Just open up that case of yours."

There was a wound on his forehead and he wore a black handkerchief round his head.

"No, not here in the street. Come along with us. Are you hungry? I'm sure we've some cake left, haven't we, Bitch?"

One of his acolytes, Bitch, was deep in a daydream. He opened his eyes. For a second, everyone on the harbour had stared at us, but now they all went back to the steady routine of their daily tasks. Time, for a moment, had stopped. And the puzzle had to be put back together all over again. The townspeople pretended not to notice our modest little enactment of a kidnapping, and suddenly the harbour square was black as a stream of pious old crones swarmed around a slow funeral procession that appeared out of nowhere, the slowest funeral procession I have ever seen. "Help!" I cried, just for the sheer hell of it. A deliberate provocation on my part. The whole town seemed to be in the square, but nobody, nobody at all was looking in our direction. Gradually, very slowly, they inched forward like some kind of nightmarish waltz, every character in the procession obsessed with his own discipline, his own tiny gestures, so that not a movement was out of place and not one of them allowed himself a single sideways glance in the intoxication of the ritual, in their desperate need to complete a dull round of deeds. I can still recall a gentleman standing just by the Crab. I bumped into him as hard as I could and he just looked the other way, casting a nonchalant, "Sorry, ladies," over his shoulder which made our little party blush. I was, in short, being kidnapped as gently as possible and propelled through this confounded funeral procession, this nervous crowd in which, for my eyes only, stood out my mother's indignant gaze. She challenged this kidnapping, she would not accept it. And I kept my eyes on her as she stood there. I could see her right at the centre of that incoherent plot, that tissue of absurdities.

"No," she said. "Anything but that."

I threw myself forwards in what was, theoretically, her direction, but which turned out to be an imaginary crowd of people standing by a cheese shop.

"Help!" I cried.

And that was it.

I have to say that, in the end, this little scene encouraged my provincial-schoolboy preconceptions.

I could tell how the scene would end. People were running around in every direction. Somehow, the accompanying band made the whole thing even more dramatic. It was fun. But everything comes to an end. I ran off through the streets of the town as fast as my legs could carry me. I made for the hills, my soul was yearning for banana fields... But this was not to be. Dullness catches up with even the best of times. My scene came to a halt. Where was the limit?

"Come here," said the old man. "Come here, lad. Have some soup."

I tell you, the whole thing was an act. Ten minutes later, there I was sweetly sipping at my bowl of soup under the watchful eyes of a little old man. Other than that it was silent. The gang burst into the tiny room of the so-called shoe seller.

"Let him finish his soup in peace!" the old man cried.

They certainly were respectful. They'd decided it would be unseemly to open my suitcase unless I was present.

"Here we are," said Bitch.

"Come on, let's have a look at this case."

I had finished the soup and sat there, sketching smiles in all directions.

"Come on, the case!" said one of them in a voice so muffled it betrayed his natural habitat of dark alleys and backstreets.

Then it all came out. What on earth could it mean? There was an extraordinarily variegated collection of shoes and ashtrays and pieces of evidence and lots of other stuff: fixtures and fittings and innumerable tins of canned cherries. Oh, and a bottle of whisky, I'm glad to add.

"Well that's all very well and good," announced the Voice, "but we still have to figure out what the whole thing is about. What do you know, what do you expect us to do for you, precisely?"

I had had time to register their faces and mark them up as future figures for my revenge. They had, in other words, got the better of me.

A couple of hours later, I recovered consciousness. They were still there, examining minute spots of blood. My instincts told me to play dead.

"So what do we do with him now?"

"We'd better ask his mother."

"Her!"

"Well, obviously the suitcase was a trap. And now the whole world has seen our little performance in the square. I tell you, we've been trapped."

As my eyes were only half-opened any idea of what was going on was quite sketchy. One of them, especially, seemed to be very excited. He looked like a monkey. He was waving a gun around and from time to time he would bring it down sharply on a walnut, cracking it open. Kids, really! But what did they want from me?

"There must be some clues here. There must be. Otherwise what are we doing in this fuckin' hell-hole?"

I was playing dead.

"Well, I tell you, it was a pretty close shave. We'd better do something, and fast."

"Christ, what a bunch of..."

"Watch out, he's listening, he isn't asleep."

"What the hell do I care?"

Only then did I realize they were speaking in all manner of different languages. And the odd thing was that I understood them all. I'm sure I did. I know that I grasped the ebb and flow of their evil thoughts.

"Let's kill him!"

"No, I don't think so."

"What then? Oh, I see, you're scared of the boss."

"The Eagle! It's been a long time since he's soared above us."

"Where is he? Here we are wasting time, wondering what he thinks, but I bet he's flown already. He's long gone."

"He can't be! What about the pancake place?"

"That's all finished with."

And here they stopped, freeze-framed. Let me describe this unique moment. One sat perched on the corner of a tiny table on which huge crabs wrestled, their claws pawing the air. Another stood at the back, not really participating because he was trying to read a map. The third man stood nearby, rummaging through the evidence, by which I mean the contents of my suitcase. And the old man, he of the soup, hung on their every word, eager to make sense of each bit of their nonsense, a real wordsmith hammering out the rhythm with a wooden spoon which, sometimes, he beat out of time. Well, someone had to mask the sound of the approaching car.

The more I think about this scene, the more confusing it becomes. Were they there yet? At any rate, they came incredibly fast, given the nature of the ground they had to cover. Well, they were there now, my mother and the others. Everyone. Only one was missing.

Half an hour later I was fast asleep in the most luxurious hotel room I have ever set eyes on. My mother was telling me stories, the sole purpose being to bore me to sleep. And, as soon as she succeeded, she'd wake me up and start all over again.

I was bound to ask her questions. The poor man was dead. I knew that already. We'd have to do without him now. I was an orphan. Like in the stories my mother was telling me (she began on another, about birds, I think). Now I'd be a true orphan.

I seem to remember they were migrating birds.

So he was dead. But... how? I fell asleep some time after midnight. I dreamt, of course, about recent events (as I am, in a way, now). My head was a confusion of facts: everything was to remain so for a good long time. The fact is I was never really able to make sense of this mass of faces, masks of suspicion that raced around my brain, endlessly multiplying ad infinitum. Once, I saw the Crab asleep. Unadulterated fear! His face was masked and as he switched from one mask to the next I could see he was crying. I awoke a couple of times.

Whenever I came to my senses, I saw my three identical faces crying in three mirrors round the room. The odd thing was, I wasn't crying, I was laughing, laughing like a mad man. You'll probably say I'm exaggerating, as usual.

"He seems like he's pretending, but he's upset really. He's deeply affected by recent events."

This was too close. I started to worry.

"He's awake!"

"Yes, madam. The fever's gone."

"His laughter was driving me mad."

"It's the shock, madam. You ought to get some rest too."

"No, Doctor, I've so much to do. I really must get a move on."

"Mum!"

"Hello, darling. Goodbye, Doctor."

I hardly had time to appreciate her new hairstyle.

"Right, lad. It's time we had a little chat. I'm Doctor Berstein. I'm on holiday and I don't intend to spoil it. So I'd like to know why none of the local doctors here agreed to take you on. You probably don't know the answer to that. If I tell you what happened to me yesterday, it might help you clarify your ideas. Apparently it can help. My name is Doctor Aloyssius Berstein, which is a funny name for a naturalized Frenchman of Venezuelan origin whose parents came from Shanghai. That doesn't interest you in the slightest, does it? Never mind, I have a feeling we're going to have plenty of time to get to know each other's life stories later on. What we really want to know now is what's been happening in that good old twenty-four hour cycle, right? That's it, lad. Yesterday, I was totally ignorant of life, as they say. Of our life, anyway, yours and mine. Let me see... yesterday certainly seems like a long time ago, doesn't it? I think I recall wanting to go out for a walk. It was early, though I'm not usually one for morning strolls. Still, yesterday, something... Well, a globetrotter like me, you know..."

He remained still, and lost for words. I knew he was making it up. He was turning everything around.

"I hope you don't mind the way I look at you? It bothers most people. The trouble is, when I was a boy, I was stricken with this particularly rare form of long-sightedness. I see perfectly well, so long as I'm looking at it more than a hundred yards away. Only the curve of the earth's surface has the power to prevent my impertinent vision. Actually, it's not all that uncommon. So, to deal with something like the matter in hand, I have to adopt this shifty look, a kind of unrespectable way of looking. People think I'm not to be trusted, but it's really just a physical thing, it's the way I look, or *see*, rather. As soon as I fix my gaze, I see, or rather, something happens, there where I see."

He was indeed blinking oddly. It was very irritating. There was something very self-satisfied about him, which is usually the sign of a coward.

"You understand what I'm saying, don't you? What I'm trying to tell you is that now, for instance, as I stare out there, I'm seeing something of considerable interest to us both... over there."

"I understand."

"I knew you would. And you've been good enough to open your mouth, I thought you'd never speak. Let's hope what I'm about to tell you will silence you for good.... Where was I? Oh, yes... there!"

Now he really was staring into the distance. It was true. There really was something going on out there, something of interest to us both. I tried to make out what he was seeing. At first, I couldn't really make out anything specific. Three farmers in their Sunday best were reading the same newspaper. A dog was toying with a dead pigeon. But then, oh yes, I could definitely see: the bar where those people, those, I'm not quite sure what to call them, those *non-tourists* had taken me. They were there now. They had the suitcase with them. And... they seemed to be repeating the scene all over again. But the only problem was I definitely wasn't there myself. I had, in short, missed an appointment. What on earth were they doing? The funeral had started all over again too.

"My poor boy, it's your father they're taking away. But, well," said the doctor, "I mustn't stray from my story. As I was saying, I decided to go for a walk very early. This is my final holiday and I didn't want to miss a minute, not even a second. So I set off towards the quay. I love walking beside a harbour, don't you? One has so many memories. Have I said, I used to live here, when I was your age? Well, I had my eyes closed anyway, remembering my lost childhood, when I heard a voice, or rather a sound like an echo from a distant past. It brought me back to reality. "Help!" the voice cried. I opened my eyes and I saw the whole thing. It was you, of course. And all those charming people were with you. They put you into a car and drove off. Well, of course, I wanted to find out what was going to happen so I closed my eyes. Have I said I possess this very sharp sense of hearing? I can hear things going on very far away, as long as they are not the same things I can see. Unfortunately, I also have two ears and they are never in tune, which means that I'm perpetually struggling to listen to two conversations that are only separate and distinct if they are sufficiently discordant. Added to which, my brain is pendular, which probably explains why I am such a melancholic."

The doctor was now basically talking to himself, so I scarcely bothered to listen to what he was saying. I was obsessed by the sight of that absurd performance, whose audience had left twenty-four hours earlier.

"As I was saying, I heard two divergent conversations though I shouldn't have been able to comprehend either. The odd thing was I could understand them both clearly. One conversation was about the other. And all the things I hadn't understood made sense suddenly, if you know what I mean."

He gave me a suitably archaic and ironic glance. Out there I saw the funeral procession fan out into a broad U-shape around the place where I had been held. They were all dressed in black, with the possible exception of my mother. But it was definitely her. My *non-tourist* friends were running around like headless chickens, coming and going with their pockets full of stuff. In the distance I heard a series of quite insolent noises: gunshots to be precise. I saw everyone scatter in different directions. A small crowd filled the great square. Shutters closed. At that instant, *the* ray of sunlight fell and was left unpunished.

In my room, the doctor was carrying on as though nothing had happened.

"One of my ears was hearing a précis of a conversation which was being carefully reiterated elsewhere: "That's him," said one of the men. "The Crab is a child-minder now, that's how low he's sunk, looking after a kid."

Then my left ear counter-attacked furiously with: "Of course we can't let him go, he saw us."

And the other ear whispered: "Where on earth can he have seen us? What has he seen? There's no point in taking unnecessary risks. Don't be absurd!"

But the left ear heard: "You must understand we'll never be able to make it unless we take him with us."

And my right ear: "I don't believe it. I'm fed up with airports. What's the point? What on earth is the point?"

And the left ear: "Diamonds."

The doctor looked exhausted and disappointed.

"That's it," he said. "That's all there is. Now I'd like to ask you a question, my boy. Where are the diamonds?"

Which was a fairly surprising question. There was a pause, the longest pause you could ever imagine. The doctor was looking out there. Then he said:

"The diamond."

I looked out over the mourning square. At the far end I saw my father, pretending, as usual, not to care. He was accompanying his own funeral. He was smiling and there, in his new set of teeth, shone a solitaire.

CHAPTER V

One week after the events that led to my father's death, I was back home, behind the reception desk. I didn't know which way to turn. At least a hundred tourists checked in every day and such numbers certainly alter such a quiet mountain place. My mother only had eyes for the visitors. We had quickly become used to the doctor's idiosyncratic digressions and we felt sorry for him because of his defective anomalies. Think! A crime! The worst! But I would have forgiven the doctor that crime, and many others, though his kindness was as treacherous as the local wine. His non-profit-making schemes caused more deaths than all the motorways combined. They were responsible for more unhappiness than the whole of Roman philosophy. But in the end, despite his sweet criminality and his cannibalistic instincts, there remained his gentle and nervous meticulousness, a kind of ponderous obsession that made him endearing. The trouble was his saviour, Timothy Moretti, who was inseparable from him. They seemed to be settling in. My mother was delighted. Well, why not? It was, after all, they who had devised a rational explanation for everything that had happened and indeed imposed a rigorous logical sequence upon events whose very nature was chaos and whose efficient cause had been overriding boredom.

Timothy Moretti, alias "The Saviour", was a Welshman, a backwoodsman. He had been one of His Majesty's honourable commissioners in the islands and a true connoisseur of lost kingdoms. He had a passion for Hong Kong. His fatal mistake had been to utter the word "poof". But that's another story, for another day.

Inevitably, there came a day when they decided they wanted to interrogate me too. They kept on asking the same old questions about diamonds, over and over again. I had not really spoken to them much at all prior to this: there wasn't any point because they realized the extent of my well-meaning curiosity. They knew I knew they were intruders.

"We know you're not telling us everything you know."

"We do and we don't," the doctor admitted.

"That's true," Timo conceded.

"But you did overhear a conversation, didn't you?" they asked.

"What, for example?"

"Tell us, will you! Just tell us anything! Who knows what might be useful."

"Useful for what?"

"Good God! You cannot refuse to cooperate with us. This is a major venture we have here."

Timo was smiling, but I could tell he was cross because his nails were white.

"I've got nothing to say. A couple of weeks ago..."

"That's a start..." said the doctor.

"Shut up! You were saying... A couple of weeks ago... what?"

Their hands were leaping around like dancers, desperate for me to say something. The trouble was, I really didn't have anything to say.

"Is that it? You're cheating!"

It was dark outside. I hadn't spoken a word in hours. I was bleeding. Someone must have hit me. The tourists were long gone. Someone must have taken care of them.

"The new boy's perfect, an absolute treat."

My mother had just come into the room. She was dressed in black. She stared at me, her lips sealed. Her voice came from elsewhere. She was playing the widow, sniggering. She had no right to do that. Her body moved gently, suffocating with self-control. And her crazed laughter died somewhere out by the kitchen.

The lady in black kissed me.

"He must be utterly confused, the poor dear. He didn't even know you existed."

"I'd forgotten," said the lady in black with a voice from beyond the grave. "Don't you recognize your auntie?" she said. "You poor darling. You'll see, I'll take you to Paris and you'll forget the whole nightmare."

But I was staring at the other woman, the one dressed in red, the blonde. Or rather the more than blonde one. My mother burst out laughing.

"Oh, poor lamb, he can't even recognize me! He didn't know my hair was whiter than snow. Oh, darling! Your mother isn't as young as she used to be, you know. My hair's been white since I was twenty."

"That's true," said my aunt, "since father's death in Tunisia."

So that was my aunt, my mother's twin sister. She seemed exhausted.

"I'm off, madam. I'll see you in the morning."

A boy about my age was watching the whole scene impassively.

"What! Already! It's much too early. Please stay for a while! He's taking over from you while you are away. Say hello."

I stared at the newcomer without really taking him in. He was all eyes for my mother.

"So the little devil told you everything?"

"Nothing!"

"That's odd. A few days ago, he talked of little else. To be honest, he was talking in his sleep."

"That might explain it, madam."

"Alright, we'll have to be a little patient," said my mother. "It's hot, give us some drinks, Antoine. We're all dying of thirst."

"What about those diamonds, Moretti?"

"Stop it, we're all sick to death of your diamonds."

No one bothered to turn the lights on. From time to time, the headlights of a huge tourist bus swept round the room carving eerie shadows of each of us. They were turned to stone.

"I've had enough!" Moretti stormed out. He was angry.

The doctor jumped up and ran after him. "What's the matter with you? Wait!"

"I suppose we must learn to take the rough with the smooth," my mother murmured under her breath.

The other boy had watched the whole exchange with a contemptuous smile. My mother stopped him in his tracks.

"Tell us what you think. What do you make of all this? I'm sure that everything you've got to say must be fascinating."

"I am, madam, very, very pleased to be working here."

Downstairs, our friends were having it out with renewed spirit. Then, suddenly, a strange kind of ceremony took place, a ceremony devised by everyone and yet no one. No one, you will see, was the cat with no name, the joker in the pack. The trump was a lure, but more of that anon.

Now the two sisters sat at the piano drumming their fingers in the air, to a waltz about to be played. And I was getting drunk in a corner, on Madeira wine. Nobody paid attention to me, engrossed as they were in making up their own little cliques.

But as soon as the waltz began, the newcomer cast off his role without the slightest noise, and, modestly keeping in time with the tune, lit up the candles. Then he started dancing by himself. Next, the doctor and Moretti returned on tip-toe and started dancing, each alone. They twirled around like that for a good while, their eyes closed. And suddenly I thought: suppose someone up there is watching? And my heart started beating faster.

The Eye, the Eye of God. Instinctively, I looked up at the ceiling. I saw the Eye. I screamed for all I was worth. Everything was shaking.

"Nobody move!"

They all looked up. The whole place had been ransacked. My toys were scattered all over the place. I looked up again, instinctively. And I saw the Eye again.

Enough, I thought, and ran up the stairs. It was quite a sight. But there was no sign of anyone, just the damage. I looked up again. Someone had opened the little window that gave onto the roof. They were all in the street now, yelling. But only one thing interested me. And that thing was hanging from the Captain's hand.

"I'm sorry, lad," said the Captain. "I'm sorry I had to do this to your cat. It was a nasty thing to do, I know, but it was really funny, really, really funny!"

Then he turned away and started to die, not exactly making a good job of it.

"I'm off, lad, I'm off on a long, long journey. Here, take your cat. I'm afraid he's come a little unstitched, but he's worth having a look at."

He was choking with laughter. He tried to stand, tottered across the floor. Then he fell down on the roof.

And I was left with a dead cat on my hands. Good God! He was right, the cat was worth a look. Gutted and embalmed, the beast reeked of lavender. Inside six, seven, eight... glass eyes had been carefully placed.

"Come here!" my mother yelled. "There'll be another quake soon. We'll have to sleep outside."

I wasn't listening. A tremendous feeling of assurance, of self-sufficiency was welling up inside me.

"The cat!" they shouted. "Give us that cat, for Christ's sake!"

Which I did.

With all my might I swung the cat by the tail and launched it into the street as hard as I could. But I had forgotten the stuff inside. Suddenly, the place fell silent. There was an enormous silence.

Down below, one of the eyes smashed to bits. A good dozen tiny diamonds spilled from the cat's innards.

We spent the rest of that evening tidying up the house. Nobody referred to what had happened but those tiny diamonds, those almost invisible diamonds, were bound to fill the rest of those lives eaten up by conceited envy.

Those diamonds were a catalyst to everything that was going to happen afterwards. From now on, every word, every gesture would have to be carefully weighed. Upstairs, the doctor and Moretti were interrogating our friend on his death bed without much success, it must be said. Not that he was abandoned to a solitary death. Worse! He spat out all he knew, adding a good hundred new pieces to our jigsaw.

Around midnight, the doctor came down to the kitchen where we had taken shelter in anticipation of more earthquakes.

"Has he said anything?" asked my mother.

"He said a great deal about you," replied the doctor, and there was nothing particularly cordial in the way he said it. "And..."

"What else?"

"Memories of Africa."

"Africa! Why Africa?"

"I gather you and your husband met *somewhere* in Africa?"

"Somewhere! That's one way of putting it!"

"Well, I gather that some political... well that you have political interests, madam?"

"Political! Me! The very idea!"

"I'm sure there's some truth in it... somewhere!"

"Enough! I don't have to put up with your insinuations. What have you got to say?"

"Nothing. I understood nothing of that Atlantis Plan. I never read newspapers and I find riddles irritating. All this talk of power struggles and coups is, as far as I'm concerned, a complete and utter waste of time. There's only one thing I'm interested in, and that's the diamonds."

"Yes," my mother said, "it's worth mentioning..."

"If you please! My father was a jeweller."

"I see. The diamonds remind you of your childhood, is that it?"

There was another quake.

"Poor man," said the doctor. "He'll never live through it. He can't bear earthquakes. He says they're the only thing in the world he's frightened of. Apart from Communism."

Moretti called: "Doctor, doctor, come here!"

They spent the best part of an hour up there with the Captain. There were three or four more earthquakes and I was fast asleep when the doctor came back.

"He wants to see the boy. No one else," he added coldly, looking at my mother. "I don't suppose he'll last long now."

There was only one candle in the room. He was giving up the ghost surrounded by shadows, our shadows.

"Come here," he said. "Come closer. We'll have a bit of a laugh now. You're a smart little lad. You catch on to more in a second than those idiots in a lifetime. Come closer and I'll tell you something. I'm very fond of you, you know that, don't you? You're one of us, I saw that right away. Well, I'm leaving now, I'm fed up with this ghastly world. You can keep your volcanoes, your rotten democracies. I'm going and I'm going in style. But before I do, I want you to promise me something. That's the least you can do, considering I killed your father. I could never bear an arse-licker. They give me the shakes. Talking of which, doctor, I'm afraid we're going to need another bottle if that's alright with you. *Rapido, outra garrafa por favor!* Don't move, laddie! Stay. And don't cry! I didn't do it, I didn't kill him. I should have done it though, who knows? Maybe it was better the way it happened. Don't cry. I even tried to save him, when I saw him hanging there over the toilet. God knows, I can't stand the sight of a hanged man. They make me sick. Stop it! What's the good of crying? I'm sure he wasn't even your real father. I want you to remember this: cowards are the root of all evil. When a coward dies, we celebrate!"

The fact is I wasn't crying at all. I couldn't.

"Here, have some of this. A drop of whisky won't hurt you. Cheers! Where was I? Are you listening?"

"Yes, Captain, you were about to ask me to promise you something."

"Oh, yes. The promise. Promise me you'll never get married. Above all, don't marry a black girl. And, here, this is for you. It's all I own. My library. I could have been a man of letters, you know? I want you to promise me something."

"You've already said that."

"This is my last request, I give you my word. I want you to read all of these books very, very carefully. If you do as I say, you'll be a very, very rich man one day, I swear. Like me. But don't forget the other promise, alright?"

"About black girls?"

"Smart boy," said the Captain. And he dropped off to sleep.

The doctor came closer. "He's still breathing," he said.

Then he took a look at my inheritance. There wasn't much of it.

"Our friend was a bookworm!"

"I'm not surprised!" said the doctor. He was livid.

He dropped a book from his hand, as if it had scalded him.

"*Mein Kampf*," read Moretti, impassive. "I've never read it. Is it any good? I mean, is it really scary?"

"*How to make good contacts and succeed in business*," the doctor announced, looking at another title. "*The Mysteries of Cathedrals*, *A noite ficou atras de Jan Valtin*, *The International Jew*, *The Petroleum Conspiracy*, *Flying Saucers and Atlantis*, *Treasure Island*."

"What? That one again?"

"*Caesar's Gallic War*, *The Cathars*, *The Third Eye*..."

The Captain was snoring, harrowingly. He was clearly in a great deal of pain.

And suddenly there was another quake. A big one this time.

"Let's get out of here," said the doctor.

They ran out of the room, but I was rooted to the ground. I was fascinated by the Captain's reaction: he was terrified. He stood and jumped around, dancing and prancing like a cat on a hot tin roof. Hanging onto the wall, he stared me in the eyes and muttered: "You're my son." He tried to laugh, but his mouth opened far too wide and he couldn't shut it.

I started laughing hysterically. He lunged at us and grabbed me by the neck, bringing his open jaws right into my face. Then he spun round and hurled himself out of the window.

Not one single house fell down in the village.

The next day it was party time.

CHAPTER VI

The police arrived three days later. They spent a long time locked in conversation with my mother and my aunt. Neither the doctor nor Moretti were at home. At last, they left. My mother had been crying. She passed by without looking at me. She shut herself in her room for ages. My aunt stayed with me. She had a serious and determined look on her face. It felt like a final farewell. Who cared? I had recovered my spirit. Everything suddenly became clear, everything made sense. The universal order of things appeared to me resplendent in new, diamond-encrusted light, which made our remote little home suddenly seem a shining and attractive place. All I had to do now was read the papers and make sure I had every detail of the whole business firmly embedded in my head.

My aunt never stopped talking. The only thing I recall now of all those things she said in her warm, husky voice is the single piercing "My very dear friend" that she uttered one day, clearly meant for someone high up inside her little head, much higher and further up than I was. When she spoke in that voice, my aunt would cross her legs and then dab on a little scent, as we shall soon discover.

"There are times," she would say, "there are times... some things... we really should, we ought to... but that's no reason not to..."

A single memory. My aunt's legs. The rest is vague, except for "See you tomorrow." And the severe: "Listen to me carefully now."

I somehow realized my mother was leaving. She was going to accompany the police. There was some discussion about all those dead bodies in the garden, and others, elsewhere. I knew that I would leave with my aunt. But, I thought, enough's enough. I decided to run away, this time without a suitcase. Here and there, I had managed to scrape together enough money to last a few months. I would make for the mainland.

I decided to go for a walk.

In the distance, I heard the companions singing the serenade of the caves. Why not pay them one last visit? Despite the rising tide, I thought I could still go deep into Polyphemus' Throat, where the winds swirled around. I had taken my storm lantern. I edged forward in the darkness. After a while, I joined in the song, the last song I heard my father sing.

"And a bottle of rum!"

"I know that song," I heard a voice say.

"Really?"

"Yes, it's a pirate song."

"Who are you?"

"We were introduced the other day."

"Oh, I know, you're the one taking over from me at the hotel."

"Well, that's one way of looking at it. You don't mind, do you?"

"No."

He was on the other side of the cave. I could see his paraffin lamp moving around.

"What are you doing here?" he asked. "I know why I'm here. I've come to kill myself. But I don't really see..."

"I'm here to think."

"About what?"

"Life. Death. Everything that's been happening to us."

"I see," he said. "Well, I don't care. Soon, I'll be gone."

"Me too," I said. "Far away."

"Not as far as me. I'll be dead."

After a bit, he began to cry. Then he chucked his lamp into the sea.

"What did you do that for? You're crazy! Where are you?"

"I'm still here. Can I ask you something very personal?"

"Go ahead."

"Have you ever loved someone?"

"I think so. My father, and my mother."

He burst into a fit of frenzied laughter.

"Me too!" he squawked. "Me too!"

"So?"

"Alright," he went on. "Tell me. You say you love your mother. That's great. Now tell me about her."

Then I understood.

I fell silent.

"I'm sorry," I said. "There's nothing to say."

"Nothing, really?"

A long silence followed. I saw him do some kind of pantomime.

Each one of his gestures made me go strangely deaf, as a mirror is deaf. The whole thing took ages, would take ages still. I don't know how to describe the peculiar quality of the silence that fell upon us. It was a silence carved in the sound waves and the music of each wave was distinct, a discernible entity. I saw how closely each of his gestures fitted a particular wave. His act began with a whirlpool corresponding almost exactly to the deep waters inside the cave. Then a huge wave bore down on us. The wind was like a slap in the face. The Throat, that deep gorge, seemed to swallow sound. The waves broke into iridescent ripples. Each fresh element of his performance would absorb the last of a wave as the cavern sank into a kind of comforting silence in which only the shadows cast by the lamp danced.

Then he jumped.

I saw him vanish into the water. His last gestures, like an echo, were almost a goodbye by shadows transmitted onto the walls of the cave. His lamp sank. And all the sounds converged onto a single A major chord, though not strong enough to drown out the sound of my enemy's voice.

"Help!"

I returned to my corner. He called out a couple of more times, his voice multiplied by the companions. Polyphemus' Throat proclaimed a full state of alert. But I was not flustered. I knew he'd never survive until the rescue team arrived. The fishermen knew how to take their time. They'd never leave a spoonful of soup to prevent fate from accomplishing its dirty deeds.

Fate, in this case me, was taking a close interest in each movement of the waves; I would have liked to preserve and crystallize every instant of his despair. My enemy only had eyes for me. He could no longer talk, he mumbled. He made a full confession. How on earth could I, a mere child, have understood so much in such a short time?

Through the mouth of that drowned child I penetrated still further into the land beyond. He whispered his feelings towards my mother, insidiously. He displayed, in his last, submerged kiss the secret they had shared. But I was smiling, I guess. I let him drown, quite simply. God, it dragged on. The expression on his face took all the pleasure out of the crime. And to ward him off, I kept on repeating: "Die! Die!"

He finally got the message. He grew calmer. His face, for the last time, was distorted into what he thought would make a suitable final kiss. He adopted a position and the currents dragged him away. This was the precise moment the fishermen decided to burst into the cave. I must have taken up a somewhat theatrical posture for suddenly the whole world burst into applause that reverberated in the gorge. At that moment a huge wave brought the bloody body of my enemy crashing back to my feet. I tried to get away but it was tangled in sea weed that wrapped itself around my limbs. I fell on him and a mouthful of freezing water escaped from his mouth.

"He's alive!" someone shouted. "He saved him!"

And another round of clapping echoed through the sleeping village.

Then he was given the kiss of life. The fishermen turned round. I was laughing. Someone had given me a drink and I was bubbling. It was such a good joke. What would the good old fishermen say when they heard, from the victim's own lips, that I had tried to kill him? I'd had enough. I left and headed back to the hotel. A car that I hadn't noticed blinded me with its headlights.

"My startled rabbit."

I recognized the doctor's voice.

"Come here. Let's hear what you've got to say for yourself. We'd better go somewhere else, the police are watching the house."

He took me to the hotel across the street. Three fishermen were drinking around the fire. They clapped when they saw me.

"You're becoming popular, I've heard."

"Nothing special. I tried to kill someone, that's all."

"Is that so?" said the doctor. "You're soaked, and you're still bleeding."

It was blood then.

"So?"

"Nothing. I just want a quick word. I've got to go to Funchal right away. I'm expected. We'll be leaving within a couple of days, I hope."

"Leaving? Where to?"

"Wherever you take us."

"Me? I'm meant to be taking you somewhere?"

"I'm sure you can show us the way, if you really want to."

"Hold on. What...? Why...?"

"Where are your books? Your father's book, I mean."

"My father's?"

"The Captain's books."

"I have no idea. They're at home, somewhere."

"Well, we'd better get them quick. Come on."

"But... I thought we couldn't get into the house?"

"It's all relative."

"Next week."

"That'll be too late. Come on, let's go now."

"I can't."

The doctor looked me in the eyes. I knew that look. That was the way the Captain had looked at me the day he died. Then, he smiled.

"I'm sorry, lad," he said, "you must be freezing, right? Sometimes, we adults can be too hard on kids. Too demanding. Sometimes, we forget children are children. Children are very fragile..."

"Yes," I said, "I'm a very fragile person, very sensitive to the cold. I'm very sleepy too. You can see that I hope."

"Of course I can. I'm a doctor, you know."

"Also, my aunt is expecting me. I'm sure she's worried."

"But, tell me if I'm wrong, your aunt lives with you."

"Yes, but she isn't allowed to touch anything. She can't take anything out of the house."

"Well of course we won't touch anything. Nothing that matters. You'll just swap one object for another that's identical. That's all."

"What object?"

"Well, nothing at all really. Just a book."

"A book?"

Gingerly, the doctor pulled a copy of *Treasure Island* out of his pocket.

"You probably know this book?"

"I haven't read it yet."

"Nobody cares whether you've read it or not, you little idiot!"

He was livid, and shaking. Suddenly, he burst out laughing.

"You know everything, don't you? I see it all now. I've been beaten at my own game, by a child yet again. I'm really stupid, much too stupid."

"I've got to go now. My aunt told me to be home early."

"But that's the whole point. It isn't early now. It isn't early any more. Why bother doing what your aunt says? What's an aunt, anyway?"

"I'm off..."

"Wait."

Except, this time it was my aunt speaking.

"Here, I've brought your jumper. It's cold out there. Now's our chance, doctor, the guard's fast asleep. He's blind drunk."

"You're an angel, madam."

"Hop in through the window, darling. I left it open. Your books are on your mother's bed. Take this."

She took the book from the doctor's hand and passed it to me. Then she kissed me. Properly. Well, that was it. Now, she had won me over. And she knew it. I ran across the street and went round the back. The policeman on guard was asleep, arms hanging, mouth wide open, like someone singing an aria. I have to say, in his favour, the moon was full that night.

In the house, the greatest confusion reigned: things had been put back in other places. Every single item had been taken out and inspected. And that was not going to be the end of it. Everything was going to be inspected again, a second, then a third time. Everything had found the most temporary home it was possible to imagine. Because I knew the house well, I moved fast, but because nothing was in its proper place, I kept bumping into things and falling over. I froze and waited for the guard to wake up. Instead of "Who's there?" all I heard was a spine-chilling chuckle.

I climbed quietly up the staircase. For the last time, I enjoyed the creaking of my childhood nights. I thought: "This isn't me, going up these stairs, it's my father, my mother. I am the Captain. All those who are absent are climbing these stairs with me." I was sure the creaking was getting louder, multiplying. I saw a shapeless pile of carefully strewn books. Obvious little marks had been left so that any unauthorized tampering with the books would be noticed. *Treasure Island* was half-hidden under *The Mysteries of Cathedrals*. I swapped the books with a degree of solemnity. A sinister chuckling interrupted me.

"Ssssh!"

There were two of them. I recognized Bitch. The other man stayed in the shadow, but his voice brought back too many unpleasant memories. He was the one who was partial to extreme solutions. He was the one who had hit me once.

"You're looking for something?"

"My books."

"Books! Let's see."

"Yes, old man, only books. We're wasting our time. You'll see what the Eagle has to say about all this."

"He'll have to come with us now."

"What for?"

"How should I know? I presume the Eagle would want to ask him a few questions."

"You aren't here to presume."

"Well, what else can we do? We can't kill him, can we?"

They stared at me. Then one of them came over and started to stroke my head.

"Listen, lad, I know who you are, but you don't know who I am, do you?"

"Here we go again," said the other man.

"That's right, here we go again. I think I have the right to tell my son who his father is, don't you?"

"Arsehole."

"Quiet!"

Someone was coming up the stairs. They took out their guns.

"You'll see what kind of a man your father is. I bet you've never seen anything like it."

"You're really sick," the other man said.

But he wasn't sick. He was dead. His mate was terrified. He shot at no one three times, then took a shot in my direction, for good measure, before jumping out the window.

I heard a few more shots in the distance. Then I fainted.

CHAPTER VII

Everything I have just told you took place in my mind during the ensuing two weeks. Deep reasoning and shallow, half-baked thinking were inextricably entwined within my head, like twin sisters squabbling. Let's just say, I had forgotten everything. I was convinced I was grown-up. And without my being aware of it, an alien and totally fabricated form of life had taken root inside me with feverish parsimony. I was determined to be this grown-up person who thought he was me.

"Let's admit you are my father," my voice whispered. "Let's also admit you've killed me. So how come your body is my wounded body?"

"I have taken over my son's murdered body," I replied with no sense of conviction.

The sky was a deep blue and somehow gave credibility to this exchange. But I was blinded by the setting sun. It made me drowsy, and my memories of the deceased soon retreated into the recesses of the house.

Where was I?

I was falling, that much was clear. I was falling and I had just shot at somebody I felt sure was also my son.

Also?

Downstairs, someone was playing the piano. I tried to get out of bed. I was walking on cloud, swept away by the waltz.

I was surrounded by spirits. I caught glimpses of myself in a receding mirror, penetrating deeper and deeper into the dark corners of the house. This house was made of doors. Through one, which was ajar, music filtered. I entered a library. My aunt was playing the piano. Moretti and the doctor were dancing. There were books everywhere. There was one book everywhere. The only book which mattered now.

"Here comes our survivor at last!"

My aunt stopped playing. She kissed me slowly.

"He'll be fine in a week. Completely cured. I knew he'd be alright. He's strong."

"My poor boy, poor thing," my aunt kept saying, "you don't know how lucky you are. You're a very lucky person."

I had no idea what they were on about. What was all this stuff about survival? I was exhausted.

"Go back to bed, now. I'll tell you what, take this book to bed with you. If you wake up and feel up to it, have a little read. It will do you some good."

I picked up the book mechanically, the one and only book. My aunt took me back to my room.

"Where's Mummy?"

"She's gone away for a little while."

"Are we going away too?"

"Not yet. We have a lot of things to clear up first."

"What kind of things?"

"Oh, you know, the treasure and all that. I'll tell you about it later. Go to sleep now."

That night, I woke up around midnight. Downstairs, they were having a furious row. Moretti was beside himself with rage.

"They can't do that! I don't care whether it's a military zone or not, I'm going there."

"...visas..."

"Who cares, for God's sake? We'll pull strings."

"...the rainy season..."

"Sir, I'm an Englishman..."

"Ripley."

"...I'm English Mr Ripley. I like islands. I love rain..."

"I can't say that I agree with you."

"Moretti's the name."

"I'm a Frenchman, Mr Moretti. I have no time for schoolboy excursions, and this is definitely one. I am, I'd like to remind you, sir, a French citizen."

"Well, I am a French citizen too, Mr Ripley, and I happen to be Jewish to boot. You probably think I like money. Well, I don't. I don't have much time for fame. Or grandeur either. When it comes down to it, there's nothing I respect quite so much as a plain, old-fashioned schoolboy excursion. Which, as you say, is what this is."

"Well, let's polish off this bottle."

They were all blind drunk, my aunt included.

"Here's to the hell of it!"

"Cheers!"

Well, that was that. They were all going off in search of treasure. But what exactly was this treasure island they kept on referring to? I must be sure to read that famous book, one of these days. I opened it. Two minutes later it fell from my hands.

Over the next few weeks, I hardly left the house. I slept all day and woke at nightfall to listen to the adults conversing. They stayed up late, endlessly talking over their plans. Bit by bit, I fitted the jigsaw together. Before going to sleep, every day, I opened the book. And every day, I gave up. There was something scary about it.

One night, they went out early. I stayed by myself and was finally able to read the book. I read it all carefully and thought I had made sense of the whole business. They were kids. I was surrounded by kids. So they wanted to go in pursuit of treasure. But on what island? What was it all about?

I heard a stone strike my window. Then another. I ran out into the corridor. I was scared. From the window in my aunt's room, I looked out into the street. There was someone down there. He whistled and threw another stone. I could see him clearly now: it was my enemy, my mother's suitor.

"Hello," he said. "Don't hide, I know you're there. I need to talk to you."

Downstairs, he hugged me.

"Thank you," he said. "They told me everything. You saved my life."

"No, I didn't," I replied. "I even tried to kill you."

He just laughed.

"You could have done. You should have done. But then I wanted to die, didn't I?"

"That's true," I said.

"Well, now I no longer want to die. I want to live and I want to save your mother's honour. I want you to know that nothing the newspapers say is true. Your mother is a fine woman. She's virtuous, and she's honest. She's a lady."

"She's gone away."

"No, she hasn't. She's right here. I'm supposed to meet up with her."

He took me down to an alleyway leading to the harbour. Across the water, a cargo ship lay moored.

"Be careful, the police are watching us. But your mother can handle that. She promised she'd be here in five minutes."

"I don't get it."

"Don't try. You'll see."

He fell silent. He seemed to be thinking. He was thinking about her. I could easily kill him now. We were at the water's edge. I knew he couldn't swim. I stood up and pushed him. He leapt back and spun round.

"You thought I'd fall in, didn't you? Didn't you?! You're just jealous. What were you trying to do? You know I can't swim and you would have had to jump in after me, wouldn't you? Well?"

"I don't like the way you refer to my mother. You should show a little more respect."

"I'm in love with her."

"Don't."

"Why not?"

"I don't know. Perhaps you're right."

"Of course, I'm right. She's the most beautiful woman in the world."

There was silence.

"My aunt's a very beautiful woman too."

"Maybe she is. But it's different. She's kind of..."

"Kind of what?"

"Well, I hope you don't mind me saying so but... I think she's a bit vulgar. You're in love with her, I take it?"

"No, I'm not. I think she's nice, that's all."

"Have you ever seen her naked?'

"No!"

"Well, how can you possibly know then?"

"Have you seen my mother without any clothes on?"

"Yes, of course."

"And?"

"I told you, she's a lady. Naked or dressed, she knows how to behave. The way your aunt does. I mean, you can't tell whether she's wearing any clothes or not. Oh, look, there she is."

My mother had appeared on the deck of the ship. She was waving a red scarf. She was saying goodbye. She was saying goodbye to my enemy.

So I pushed him into the water, and whilst some others rallied round to give him an undeserved hand, I went home to reread the final chapters of the book.

PART TWO

CHAPTER I

From the spectacular mass of astronomic observations (and we'll realize immediately that those laborious descriptions of the movement of stars and those more discrete allusions to Greek mythology conceal, simply, the bodies of men and women peppered by the early morning *spraying* of the 21st May 1967, a massacre which marked the destiny of a tropical republic in search of an identity and which, in spite of that, has kept, until today, the name: *Treasure Island*), from that corpus of numbered stars, and milky numbers, I retained the following proposition (page 35): "Behind each best-seller, behind each children's book with some success, a sacred text is concealed," and further (page 97): "The sky is the real treasure map," and still further: "It's for us to find the relationship between the movement of the stars and the adventures within a fairy tale."

Robert Louis Stevenson's book had been scrutinized, read and re-read a thousand times. It has been used as a model for a map which was to lead us in search of an island where (the doctor thought he knew) that cave representing the sky was located. In that sky, you will have guessed, the stars and planets were represented by diamonds, real diamonds. Where could one have gathered such a quantity, such a variety of stones to represent, even approximately, the celestial vault? The doctor thought he knew but he concealed his intuitions with sneering laughs and memory lapses.

It was a good idea. For the time being it was only a suspicion, an inspired intuition, Moretti repeated. It is unfortunate that the most brilliant ideas are whimsical and that they think it's good to choose, as definitive home, the heads of the most mediocre of men. Yes, Timothy Moretti was stupid and the doctor had been convinced that it was irrefutable data: the idea was that of a genius but the author was a total moron. And that was very convenient for the doctor's business, for he was a man full of genius but short on ideas. That said, they had trouble to find partners for their enterprise.

"No, no, no. It's not true. It's impossible, it's ridiculous and fucking idiotic."

The curser chewed his words with the help of some strands of tobacco from the islands that he rapidly pretended was chewing gum each time someone scowled at him.

"I understand he doesn't agree and that surprises me," Timothy said dryly.

"We're facing what is called a Frenchman," the doctor whispered. "He confuses logic with good sense."

"I find the book diverting, often funny. From a strictly military point of view, it says very accurate things. The very idea that such a book can hide a secret delights me."

The captain followed the hand movement of the others and he was right, the words told of the delights to come, their hands were already counting the dead; each dead one was worth a diamond, there was therefore a fortune to weave in arabesques. A flying carpet ready to take off in spite of those damned chewing gums.

"...the book is stuffed with mistakes and contradictions."

"...that's part of its charm."

"Do you want to know where that island is located, according to the information in the book? Well, it's not far from Scotland."

"Charming."

"With the information given by the book, you could never manage to draw a map."

The doctor was not listening; it was clear he must have heard voices in the distance threatening him. As far as knowing if they came from the past, the next world, or the harbour, it was impossible to guess (except that they were actually devouring his brain). He made an enormous effort to come back to us. After a wince that crossed the sky to settle on the first page of a newspaper burning in the chimney, he said painfully:

"We have enough information to believe that the marvellous delirium of Mr Moretti is consistent."

"Tell him we are convinced, although the book is born of Mr Stevenson's fertile imagination, that others later have used the information from the book to hide real treasure."

The doctor managed to forward inside himself a semblance of an echo from his strange beyond-the-grave.

"I think we have insisted too much on the fact that..."

And he sank into oblivion.

"But do you know everything there is to know, captain?"

"No."

"There you are. You need to know, don't you? Even a child like this one could understand."

But he was not looking at me. He was watching the fire. For an eternity the face of a child was burning. Now the doctor hummed a pirate song.

"They're singing there," he said with a malevolent voice.

"I've heard that, at the end of his life, Stevenson used his book as a magpie uses a nest to hide his very famous collection of old coins. It's a well-known fact, it was in the papers. Several modern pirates have used that book to hide their treasure. And more. For a while now, they began to suspect the existence of a megalo-map of treasure which would reveal, once and for all, the total number of places where the three hundred and sixty five treasures of the world would be hidden."

"It makes one dream," the captain said, unconvincingly.

At that moment, the doctor stood and ran away. His distant voice remained with us for a long time.

That voice was the famous flying carpet I was thinking about earlier, those threads tried to strangle us while the voice made its way in our ears, whispering breathlessly:

"I'm already far away. Where? I don't know. My right ear summons me to the harbour, where the blameless killers are waiting for me, my left ear summons me to the mountains, where the one-eyed killer is waiting for me, alone. Tomorrow's papers will relate that double homicide. Beware that my death, if it is multiplied by a double identical murder, will bring me back among you with my very last life unscathed.

Above all I certainly should not look to death for a solution that would put that last life in danger. Yes, I know, the echo of my story won't tell you much, except that I'm already far away. I've always tried to escape through my double ear.

"Until now, what I heard on the right was equidistant from what I heard on the left. I therefore knew the dimensions of my prison. It's only three months ago that my acoustic territory started to create echoes with words endowed with unison. That resonance made me light, somehow, and above all, sparing of words, I mean to say that at the moment, only harmonies break through my limits and (sometimes) manage to drag me away from that kind of torpor you mistake for courtesy. That heartbreaking music draws me at the same time to my left ear's side and to my right ear's side. However, each time, I have to choose. The worst thing that could happen to me. Then, we live in the provinces and all that's said around us affects me. All of those who slander me, call on me. I look around me and the fall point of each of my extremes asserts itself and lasts forever in an avenging word. I am lost."

We saw the doctor reappear. It was the first time I saw him drunk and his delirium had the ability to drag out of the Captain the only kind word I'd ever heard him utter:

"Doctor, you are a poet," he said. "I know because I understand everything you say. Yes, sailors and poets have many things in common. Everything you say is at the same time very beautiful and very useful. I also live like a prisoner of what I hear from the right and from the left. I, too, I ran myself down mercilessly. I live surrounded by plotters and murderers with petty minds. Your speed convinced me at least on one point. You and I, we would be capable of preventing any mutiny. Yes, doctor. I'll be back, and we'll talk about it again."

"You surprise me," Moretti said. "You believe in mutiny in the twentieth century?"

The captain swore and left.

That's when the doctor appeared. He was pale and the wound was hanging on his face. It looked like a squid drowned in a pot of jam.

"Your wound is very handsome, doctor," Moretti said.

The chiaroscuro and the distant storm were definitely making our souls tolerant and curious.

"They tried to kill me."

"Who?"

"A cat," the doctor said. "I was drawn towards the kitchen with the help of an explosive cat. I managed to throw it through the window before it burst, the poor thing."

"I didn't feel the explosion."

"It coincided with the thunder."

"There are more and more coincidences in this business."

"There," the doctor screamed, "there it is again."

From the living room door, a black cat watched us closely.

"Let's go, quick, it's going to explode again."

"Do you think it's capable of exploding seven times?"

"My God, another's coming, and another."

How many were there? Three? Four?

"Seven cats. They are all going to explode, quick."

They ran away.

I was left alone, surrounded by famished cats. They went towards the chimney and began miaowing as they watched the fire. There were only six. Thus I felt obliged to follow their example. They didn't pay attention to my presence. They were watching my photo burn in the chimney.

It was me, and it was not. In an old newspaper, the picture of someone who looked like me was vertiginously burning with an improbable smile. It was my father. The newspaper article was perfectly readable. I saw my father's photo leaning over and reading upside down what was written. I followed his eyes:

"Yesterday evening an extremely serious incident happened in a Lebanese pizzeria which definitely brought into disrepute one of the most famous places in our island. Indeed, on Wednesday the 11th, just before noon, a man in his thirties took a seat and asked for food. A menu was brought to his table. On the card, instead of the menu, the names of several persons the police were looking for were written. That's the dish of the day, the waiter said, pointing to the very name of the customer who, realizing now he had fallen into a trap, started to shoot in all directions, wounding a few passers-by. The manager of the restaurant had to finish him off with a hunting rifle."

The photo of my father pulled a face and started laughing.

"Who were you? The murderer or the murdered?" I asked, as if party to the crime.

"It was on your birthday," he said. "I had bought some fireworks. You do like fireworks, don't you," he asked, suddenly worried.

"I love them," I said.

"Well, happy birthday," he said, before disappearing.

The cats exploded gaily.

"Thanks, dad, what a wonderful idea."

"I'm happy to hear that."

"I didn't know fireworks could miaow. It set my teeth on edge. That must have cost you a lot."

"A lot."

"Thanks again. Oh, my God, we forgot to call my mother. She's going to be furious."

"I'm afraid so."

"We'll say nothing?"

"Okay. Omertà."

"Omertà."

CHAPTER II

I had just finished reading the *Confessions of a Woman in Africa* when an explosion shattered the window. A milky white tongue stirred into the storm clouds. The town came to life. Everything was radiant that morning. But I had lost my left eye. My uncle came to visit me in hospital. Since childhood he had made a habit of getting himself into trouble. He informed me I was liable for compensation.

"An eye," he said, "is probably worth a tidy sum." He winked rather more laboriously than was tactful under the circumstances.

So now I only had one eye. That only fired my taste for reading further. Despite the censors, I managed to get hold of all the newspapers and thus discovered that the woman I loved most in the world had a son. He had been severely burnt in an accident and had little chance of survival.

It was my duty to pay him a visit.

As far back as I can remember, I have always been very good at absconding, so getting out of hospital was child's play and, by midnight, I was at the clinic for the wealthy.

The burnt boy was lying there, on the third floor. He had already had three operations. His breathing was difficult and was interrupted by fits of laughter. His eyes moved around, but he didn't seem to be able to focus on anything. He didn't notice me. I did what I thought best: I sat at the end of his bed and began reading to him aloud from the *Confessions of a Woman in Africa*.

"The stars are my homeland," the woman stated by way of introduction. A chance encounter with a late eighteenth-century novel had led her to discover the origins of her family.

The book in question was written in appalling pidgin, full of hilarious coinages. It told of a journey to Mali undertaken by two French gentlemen in about 1770. They were accompanying a party consisting of three Egyptians, a Portuguese and two Maltese. They carried a coffin that they hurriedly buried on arrival, calling a meeting of tribal chiefs and announcing their intention to excavate a hillock near the tomb. They were charged a considerable amount for permission to build a temple there and they set to work immediately. First of all, they dug a series of circular and concentric ditches. Then they started building a small fort. It took them the whole year to complete the work.

Unfortunately, an epidemic wiped out most of the expedition so that only the two Frenchman, and their one Maltese companion, survived. They decided to leave. As they had established excellent relations with the natives during their stay, before their departure, one of the chiefs offered them a young princess as a gift. They promised to take her to Europe and find a prince who would marry her. Furthermore, they promised to return within a year bringing a European princess for one of the African princes to marry.

As soon as they were gone, the whole story was forgotten. The remains of their fortified temple were rapidly swallowed up by the sand. A few years later, the natives saw a caravan approaching composed of young, bare-footed soldiers escorting a young, blonde girl. She must have been about fourteen years old and her retinue not much older. As soon as they arrived they played a peculiar game of blind's man buff, ignoring the hunters who had come out to greet them. Then they asked if they could have some water and drank it mixed with a strange, blood-coloured cordial. They chatted away amongst themselves and laughed a great deal. The hunters were astonished at such self-confidence. Eventually, the young soldiers decided it was time they had a nap. They slept right through till the following day.

That morning they were awoken and given a frugal breakfast. At last, the girl spoke to the hunters. She gave a speech in their own language that she had previously taken the trouble to learn by heart.

As soon as she had finished, she was astonished to find herself led away and forced into a hut where she was whipped for the entire day. Then, stripped naked and dressed in a tunic whose design (as was learnt much later) was decorated with a representation of the celestial vault, she was taken to a nearby village and given in marriage to one of the hunters. As for the boys who had accompanied her, they were put to death a few days later, following the instructions the girl had unwittingly given.

She lived amongst the hunters for one year. Pregnant and undoubtedly in a state of extreme despair, she decided to escape. For five whole days and nights, she walked across the desert. Then, on the sixth day, she gave birth to a baby girl whom she buried alive at the foot of a dead tree. After spending the following night in prayer, in the morning, she slit open her veins. At dusk her body was devoured by hyenas.

The following night, the hyenas came back to the spot. They must have sensed the presence of the buried baby for they dug it up. Nobody will ever know whether the child was suckled by the hyenas or rescued by a band of marauding thieves. The fact is that by the time she returned to her father's village to avenge herself, she was already the subject of a thousand legends and innumerable songs praising her for her skill in healing and for her control of the firmament. She entered the village escorted by a pack of blind hyenas. Her laughter silenced the drums. When she ran towards her father, everyone thought she was going to kiss him. But the princess cut off his head and clasped it in her hands. She breathed into his lips and threw it high in the air. Then an extraordinary thing happened: from her father's lips came such a horrendous howl that everyone laughed. Then there was an eclipse and no one can now deny that it was the head of the hunter, and not the moon, which eclipsed the sun. The truth is they never found the slightest trace of the head. The body, after having been torn to pieces by the hyenas, was scattered in seven different directions, corresponding to the seven cardinal points marked out by the earlier expedition, at the time the temple was built.

Once her task was accomplished, the girl and her hyenas vanished. Nobody had dared hold her back. Three years passed. A hundred hymns were composed in her honour. Towards the end of the rainy season of the third year, a rumour was heard that the young princess had disguised herself as a warrior to take up arms against the slave-traders plaguing the country. Hunters from every part of the land left their villages to join her army. Two years later, the rebellion suddenly petered out. The hunters dispersed and, in a ceremony reminiscent of the last deed of the army which had, five centuries earlier, defeated the Sultan's troops, they committed suicide, each one individually defying the Governor's superior forces.

As for the princess, this is what is said in a song the griots are still performing today:

"There was once a terrible battle in which the heads of no less than three thousand slave-traders were chopped. And during the course of it, the hunters discovered a beautiful black slave girl hiding behind the carcass of a camel. It was decided she should be married to one of the oldest chiefs of the clan (marriage being an indispensable part of the procedure by which a female slave might be freed). But the head of the hunters intervened. When it was pointed out that he already had four wives (they knew their general's true sex, but tradition demanded that he should marry at least three times), he declared that, if they dared refuse to grant him that slave, he would abandon them all and leave forever. Then they noticed that the captive girl was almost identical to their general, like two peas in a pod.

"The two of them became inseparable. Issa (for such was the liberating princess' name) was infatuated with Muna, the captive. The story of their unnatural love was sung by griots and provoked, within a few months, the fury of the tribal coalition. Issa's army was quickly routed by its enemies. That first catastrophe coincided with the beginning of a three-year drought. At the same time an epidemic decimated the population. There could be no doubt about it, Issa and Muna's love had provoked the wrath of the stars. It was decided that they should be sacrificed. It was only on the day appointed for the sacrifice that the officiates discovered that Muna was a man. He declared that his mother had been an African princess, married to a courtier at Versailles (who was in fact an actor playing the prince's part in operas performed in honour of the king) and that, in exchange, a princess (needless to say she was really a young actress from the same company) had agreed to go to Africa to marry one of the princess' brothers. Muna was the son of the black princess given to those two French travellers long ago, and Issa, daughter of the actress whom they had sent to Africa in exchange. They were, in short, cousins.

"After an interminable debate, during which there was much discussion of twin constellations, it was decided that Muna should be freed and the young lovers left the kingdom of hunters."

Now it happens that the woman I loved most in the whole world, that "woman of Africa", was adamant she was the great granddaughter of Issa.

And that should have been the end of the story, but there was an epilogue, clearly written by someone who didn't share the same taste for flowery and flamboyant metaphors. In the epilogue, it was specified that seven children were born to Issa and Muna, three boys and four girls, none of whom outlived their third birthday. The sickness to which they succumbed was nameless for no one else caught it. According to the author of the epilogue, these children became dry and granular, gradually turning to dust so that within a few weeks showing no sign of physical or moral discomfort, they simply vanished into thin air to be borne away by the wind. Sometimes, their faces remained suspended in the air, like pollen, and they would turn phosphorescent at night so that (for there was something eternal about the apparition) they could easily be mistaken for stars. Often, too, glow-worms joined these grains of phosphorence so that the faces of these dead children appeared in the skies and, to the great terror and delight of the peasants, their sardonic smirks were visible high above the surface of the earth. Issa and Muna decided not to have any more children. They lived together for another thirty years, wandering from village to village, Muna singing and Issa recounting stories.

One day, an old hunter begged Issa to tell him the longest story she knew. She had never before been called upon to tell a story whose digressions would have justified more than one hour's attention, so she decided to gather all the stories and combine them with the adventures of her own itinerant life. She started, and as the narration progressed, she found new stories being born, as if they were there on her lips, stories that lived and died in the span of her performance. Fascinated, the hunter called all his children and all his wives together. They remained thus, transfixed by the old woman who was giving birth to her stories before them. From time to time, Issa would pause for an hour to sleep or to eat. Two or three weeks passed in this way. Then three or four months. Towards the end of the fourth month, Issa realized she was pregnant and about to give birth. No one had paid any attention to her pregnancy, so great was their hunger for her stories, so dizzy their fascination with their boundless range.

Muna, alone, had seen everything and understood everything. He was privileged to witness the mystery of a woman made fertile by the power of her own fables. And although he knew most of his wife's stories already, he too had been fascinated by the new developments she had imagined. He cried, he laughed, he delighted in the picaresque adventures of Issa and Muna. One night, about a month after Issa had begun her marathon, Muna sensed that the tent was full of newcomers. They were invisible, but could be heard, felt and breathed. Muna had trouble accepting that they were his own dead children scattered through the heavens. Yet there they were, hanging onto their mother's every word. And furthermore, they had returned for good, an attentive constellation to Issa's epic. The story-teller breathed them in, they became the breath of the story, they moulded the tone of her heroes' speeches and tickled her audience with moments of laughter and moments of fear. They, too, had made their elderly mother fertile once more.

Issa continued to recount her epic for some months. Her pregnancy became common knowledge, but no one was surprised. It became another part of her narrative. Twelve, fourteen months passed.

Issa's fame spread abroad and pilgrims came from all regions and further afield. The town changed its name. Now it was known as "the city where stories float." Two years passed. During the rainy season of the third year, Issa felt she was about to die. She searched for a way of ending her story, but it was too late: with the rain myriad tales sprang to her lips. She realized her stories were killing her. To avenge herself, she decided to kill them off in turn. She fell silent. The whole village fell silent. For one whole day everything was quiet. The rain stopped, thunder rolled away. People in the audience slowly realized they had become mute too, irremediably mute. They too realized Issa's stories had paralyzed their tongues forever. Issa had been dead for a week but the hunters, their wives and children were still sitting there, motionless, neither eating, not drinking. They were letting themselves die.

And then the child cried.

Muna stood up. He opened his wife's belly with his sword and delivered the infant. He held it high for the hunters to see and proclaimed: "Here is my son, the son of my children. Here is my father and grandfather. I shall call him *Infinity*. The whole village burst out laughing and their laughter seemed to go on for forever. They all started talking at once, for they had all become storytellers. From that moment, their village would be called "the village of storytellers."

Muna and Infinity disappeared. They were never seen again."

That was the tale of the woman of Africa. She claimed that Infinity was her grandfather.

It was almost three in the morning when I stopped reading.

"I'll be back tomorrow night," I said. "Goodbye."

I was pleased with my night's work. In my own way I had taken my revenge.

CHAPTER III

As promised, I returned the next day, and for two days after that. I read him the whole of the *Confessions of a Woman from Africa* and, as I was reading, I could see him staring at the hole where my eye should have been. When, at last, the book was finished, I felt obliged to offer him some sort of explanation.

"Well, that was about your mother," I said.

"My mother?" he asked.

He was again staring at my missing eye.

"The Eye of God," he said, sneering.

I, the sole inhabitant of a cavern of crystal ice, decided I'd had enough. The African woman's story had struck a chord in me far deeper than any of the recent events in my own life. I had to go and look for her, I was in love with her, I hated her. I resented her, especially her eyes.

"When he saw the eye, he tried to hide. Now he inhabits it," said a voice from beyond the grave.

It was true. All the figures drawn on the walls of so vast a cave resembled watching stars. Diamonds disgraced by clever lighting and set among soup-bowl skulls, diamonds praised by shouting (but was this not I, shouting, is this not me, imitating the cries of dying men?), these it had been decided would henceforth constitute "a treasure."

"When he saw himself in the mirror, he started screaming..."

"What do you mean?"

"He is frightened by the sight of his eye, doctor. I wish we had found a more suitable colour."

"What colour?"

"Green."

"You're kidding!"

"This is the best we could find. There's no cause for alarm."

Around me a giant shell began to spin, the drawings on its walls accentuating the whirlpool effect and dragging me upwards. It was not, in fact, a shell at all, but a cathedral dome and I was floating up to the sky, up to the light of a piercing eye. Dark stones were dropping onto my head from the very centre of the eye. No, not stones, but birds decimated by the heat of a diamond. What diamond was this?

"He keeps on saying diamond, doctor."

"Quite right too. It's worth a fortune."

"Why? Do you think it's a real one?"

"Of course, my friend, of course it is."

"He's about to wake up, doctor."

They were both there. The doctor and another person they were also calling the doctor.

"Forgive me, child, this is the best we could do. You will have to get used to it."

I saw my face reflected in a mirror. I couldn't help noticing that the glass eye now embedded in the pale features of my face was staring at me. It could see something else inside me.

"He's off again, doctor."

"I've never seen anything like it! He's being hypnotized by his own eye."

"Well, it isn't exactly his own, is it?"

"Whose is it then?"

"It's on loan. It's a temporary measure, till we find a more suitable colour."

"He's a lucky fellow. It looks very sincere to me… his eye, I mean."

"Stop it, doctor."

A portly man, over six feet tall, walked into the room. He was laughing.

"Well, how is our little hero doing?"

"Now son," said the doctor, "I want a word with you."

"Yes," said the other man. "We want to know what you were doing there."

"He was reading."

"We know that. But why did you do it? I mean, one doesn't burst into a dying man's room, simply to read him extracts from his mother's erotic memoirs. Not quite the right thing to do, is it?"

"It was for his own good."

"Oh, really? And what makes you think that? He's dying, you know."

"Yes, and a good thing too," I replied.

"Well, that's a good one. That's very nice, isn't it?"

"He tried to kill me."

"I'm not surprised," said the doctor. "He always did have a slightly peculiar sense of humour."

"He tried to kill me twice."

"Do you know why?

"Because I was in love with his mother."

"What, at your age?"

"I'm fifteen."

"Exactly. I mean she's nearly forty."

"This is beside the point. I think there's something he wants to hide at all costs."

"I'm not so sure."

"There was a diamond in his left hand when we found him."

"So that's what it was," I said. "Well, I've got nothing to say. He gave it to me."

"He can't have! He can't even move."

"Yes he can. He threw an ashtray at me."

"Oh well, that's different then."

"It makes no difference whatsoever, doctor."

"So that's him!"

A woman had crept silently into the room. She stood behind a screen so I could not see her properly. In her hands, she held the manuscript the woman I love had written.

"Have you read it?" asked the doctor.

"It's awful. I had no idea my sister was leading a life of... of..."

"It's quite scandalous," the other man concurred, " but I'm absolutely sure that it's only fiction."

"That's even worse!"

"I mean she's practically boasting, isn't she? She shows no remorse whatsoever."

"I must say, I find that aspect relatively reassuring, except..."

"I know what you're going to say."

"The erotic scenes are a decoy, I'm sure."

"This gets worse and worse."

"Actually, it's rather like life, isn't it?"

"I think there's an entirely respectable motive concealed in those memoirs."

"How awful!"

In the distance, their voices were growing more and more excited. My eye focused on them. They were talking at the foot of my bed. I found myself trying to get up as they stopped dancing. I caught a glimpse of myself half-hidden behind their forms frozen as if in expectation. A mirror stood in my path.

"He's asleep. He's delirious," they whispered.

"No, he isn't. He's looking after himself, that's all."

"He's looking after his eye."

"Look, doctor, come over here. This is fascinating. Come closer, closer still. Look at his eye."

"How very curious."

"What is it?"

"It looks like there's a tiny figure observing us from within the eye."

"What is it?"

"An earthworm."

"Disgusting! Why does one always have to put up with nakedness in hospitals?"

"Pay no attention, madam, he's only fifteen. At his age, an erection has no object."

I thought my eye was spinning, would go into orbit. Everything seemed to be going faster and faster. Now I was spinning giddily about the bright room.

"It's not a worm at all. It's more like a bee, a bee encased inside the glass. Or rather..."

"Say it."

"An eye."

"Another eye!"

"This one's a machine. We must open it up. Help me, doctor."

"Stop, be careful. He bites."

"Hey! What do you think you're doing? You can't just interfere with the patients like that! Get out!"

I slept all day long. They woke me up to discharge me. When I returned to my uncle's house, there was a note pinned to the door. My uncle had gone. On a very long journey. Or so it seemed.

I never believe in messages with few characters. This message didn't spell anything at all, no hand had written it. It was penned by nobody. So I decided to go round the back. The house had been, quite anonymously, burgled. For no reason, for no purpose, in a half-hearted way. Nothing was missing, not even my uncle. He was going about his business as usual. My uncle was a man of his word and had spent his entire life trying to understand what that word meant. He had, I'm sure, learnt it before he was born. The word was *money* and its representation, the hand that sees, was always nailed on the kitchen door. But now it was gone. The only thing the burglars had bothered to take.

"They were looking for money," he giggled, "but all they found was the representation."

"Did you write that message?" I asked.

"Was it written by someone left-handed?"

"Hard to say."

"Then I did," he confirmed from the top of his pyramid. "What did the message say?"

"It said you were going away."

"Far away?"

"Yes, rather."

"Then it was me."

"Are you leaving?"

"I suppose so."

At last, he turned on the light. I could see he was dead scared. He knew his life was in danger.

"I haven't done anything wrong. I didn't see anything," he exclaimed.

"What would you have liked to have seen?"

"Nothing."

"Well, I'm not surprised. How could you have seen anything then?"

"Explain to me why they came, then?"

"Who's they?"

"The one-eyed man and his friends. Why did they want to talk to me? Why did they give me this? They should have taken everything away, stolen things, instead of which they gave me this. I'm sure it's a fake but it doesn't make the rest..."

"What rest?"

"The real ones, I presume."

"Well?"

"I swallowed them."

"Just like that."

"With my soup. One spoon for daddy, one spoon for mummy."

"Was there a little old man with them?"

"Yes, he was the worst."

"And the one-eyed man?"

"The man with a green eye?"

Then he looked at me for the first time. He had finally found a reason for his fear.

"Like you," he said. "They should have taken everything away, instead of which they gave me lots of things."

"They were counting on you being afraid," I said, to fill the silence yawning in the pit of his stomach.

"I'm not scared. I just want to know, that's all. They came here and searched the house. They could have taken everything away, but they didn't. I went white and they thought that was very funny."

Now he was obsessed by the sight of my eye and I was obsessed by his stare.

"You've come here to kill me, haven't you? I've done something very stupid, I've told you my secret. You know I carry a fortune on me and so you think, why not? Make the most of it. Well, go on then. What are you waiting for?"

He had grabbed a knife and was waving it around in the air.

"Uncle, for God's sake, give me that knife."

He closed his eyes. How had he managed to hurt himself? He started yelling:

"Help! Help! My nephew's killing me!"

He jumped from chair to chair. Frankly, it was hilarious. Then he fell onto the floor.

"Well done, Captain," I heard a child's voice say.

"Now we've got to clear up this mess."

"Yes, my uncle's a coward." I said.

"Is that why you were trying to kill him?"

"I should have. Just give me a hand now, let's clean up all this."

"I thought only children had shit like this! It's really nice, look at these colours!"

"Isn't this lovely shit, Captain?"

"There's nothing lovely about it, except the diamonds."

"Does one always have to go through this to get diamonds?"

"Yes, and it doesn't always work."

I took some of my uncle's money and gave him a note.

"Thanks," said the boy. "And thank you too, Captain."

"Take it."

"What? This too?"

He stared at the diamond suspiciously.

"Just wash it well. You'll soon get rid of the smell."

"I don't believe you, Captain."

"How do you know I'm a Captain?"

"Your eye."

"Right."

CHAPTER IV

One assumes that the young fireman must have found the blinding mist of his wedding morning quite arresting, if only because of the one-eyed and tubular grace of the hosepipes. The first thing he did, upon seeing his fiancée's dress in such a state of disorder that she was almost naked for all the assembled binocular-clad humans to see, an occasion that enormously pleased the disabled patients standing at the flaming windows, was to light a cigarette, thus precipitating the beginning of an ephemeral fire.

It's true that firemen attract fire but I would never have thought that the mere act of lighting a cigarette could provoke such an array of obscene amputations. Well-behaved as I am, my natural inclination would always be to close my eyes but, possessing only one eye, I felt it my duty to repeat the operation and, in between two blinks, I had seen: the fiancée dowsed by her husband's colleagues, running along with her one good leg about its artificial twin, whilst the assembled company of invalids waved their crutches and other bodily bits in ecstasy; a group of veterans of the African war tore open the modesty of their shirts to reveal bullet scars, as the one and only genuine amputee stood by yelling and frothing at the mouth. All this, on the very threshold of the crime scene, outside my own home.

They had, of course, shut down the neighbourhood a few hours previously and the engagement party was nothing but an excuse. The fire brigade's artificial rain could not conceal the real downpour which was now beginning in earnest.

I decided to abandon my position at the centre of all this activity and slip between parallel rains that never met.

I was safe, or so I thought and, if I had been wise, I should have vanished forever. But it was not to be for the indescribable smell of an oriental pizza reached my nostrils.

And so the other one-eyed creature, the genuine article, approached me in a truly fraternal manner. He was gently leaning over a masterpiece of ocular pizza whose unique egg flatly reflected the shuddering humanity of my crass person.

"Welcome," said the one-eyed man, not bothering to look at me. "I assume things are really hotting up out there, aren't they?"

"Yes," I replied.

"I don't think underwater weddings should be allowed, do you?"

"I should say thank you," I said grudgingly.

"Why?"

"This is a nice eye."

"Oh, well!"

He had gone pale.

"You're going a bit fast, aren't you?"

"That's nice for him."

"Is he dead yet?"

"Twice over."

"I see. It wasn't me."

"That would have been too stupid."

"Wouldn't it? As a matter of fact, I never kill."

"I'm glad to hear it. I wish I could say the same. Well, you see what I mean."

"Do you want a pizza?"

"That's the only reason I came all the way here."

"I don't believe it."

"I know you don't."

Huddled in a corner, four men wearing ties were blinding me with their glittering rows of rings.

"You can have your book back. It's immoral, but it's fairly instructive."

"Give it to me."

"Eat something first."

As the fireman's wedding drew to a close, people

ceremoniously drifted out of the pizzeria. Other fires attracted the crowd up in the hills. It was all very festive.

"So, you want to leave," said the one-eyed man.

"Yes, Captain."

He flew into a rage.

"Never, ever call me that. Understood?"

"Understood."

The ties were clustered in a hum of surreptitious whispering, indispensable to the start of any serious undertaking. It was like a fight except there was no sign of a knife, no sign of violence, but some kind of masculine dance, a settling of accounts.

"They're training," said the one-eyed man.

"For what?"

"Oh, all sorts of things."

"How can they do all sorts of things at the same time?"

"That's their Achilles heel. I wish I could do something about it. I don't have the energy any more. We need people like you. We need young, uncontaminated idealists. They have no faith any more, they've lost it. Come on," he added, "I want to show you something."

In the attic there were rows and rows of wonderful shoes. Somehow they spelt humanity.

"I love shoes," he said, "I consider them important somehow. I think I left my childhood behind in that attic. Each one of those shoes, even the tiniest, is like a disillusion following me around."

A fierce, limpid roar burst forth from the wide open jaws of the big boots. It was like a room in aspic.

"Here it is."

He had covered the most salacious pages of the book in reams and reams of scholarly notes and devastating figures. I assumed all the scribbling was just a pretext to hide better the nudity of the book's characters.

"The first thing that jumps to mind is the recurrence of the word *member* and the insistence on the number seven. It is obvious it refers to the seven members of our association."

"Only seven?"

"Well, seven founder members, out there. Then we had to have more, to spread the cost."

"He knows everything."

"Who? The boy?" There was nothing pleasant in his laughter. "Who cares? He's dead."

"Not yet, he isn't."

"I know, but he's a monster now; and he's far too pretentious to dare to venture into the streets with a face like that."

I opened the book at random. The passage I found was, as usual, about an orgy: several men and one woman. There were indeed seven of them.

"The woman counts for zero," said the one-eyed man.

At first, three men went with her, then two. In the end, she was alone.

"320."

"Then she took one man only, then two, while the other three looked on."

"Three men watching means you have to divide the total by three."

And thus the figures, disembodied now from any association with character or fiction, took on a gloriously illuminating meaning. Our twin eyes literally devoured them. These numbers meant diamonds, treasure and certain death. They meant goodbye, immediately. And safe journey.

"Do you understand what this means?"

"Yes, Captain."

"Those idiots think the book is everything. But we must take both books into account, otherwise God knows where we'll end up."

"We?"

"You're coming with us."

"Are you sure?"

"You don't have any say in the matter."

"I can believe that."

"They've got our late friend Molina's copy, annotated by him, and we've got Lily's, with your father's notes."

"My father?"

"I'm sorry, I keep on forgetting you're new to this business."

"That means, I've got to be..."

"You're our candidate."

"Candidate? What does that mean?"

"You'll be there, you'll be the go-between."

"There's just one thing I need to know. Was the boy who was burnt going to..."

"Be your stand-in."

He was an expert at perverting the most obvious situations.

"I want you to sleep here tonight."

"I can't refuse?"

"Correct."

But he seemed to have lost interest in me. He looked around nervously, like a child looking for its parents. Hoarder of memory-rats poured forth from the mouths of the shoes and nibbled away at the past – a tight crowd, bursting at the seams of its billowing tailcoats struck up a vagabond melody. The rigorous discipline of their playing quite overcame the one-eyed man and he fell in, obediently, with the music of these lyrical rodents. How many players did the orchestra of his memories require? As many, no doubt, as there are diamonds in the skies of that Treasure Island. They are to be numbered in terms of tricks, a closed but enthusiastic number. The mouse hymn gathered a multitude in the one-eyed man's brain and here and there stabbing sharp cries pierced the empty socket of his other eye.

His delirium lasted till dawn.

I woke up to the stench of my own vomit. He was gone. By mistake, perhaps, they had locked me in. I found a staircase leading onto the roof. A stiff little door finally opened out on to the reeking, pitch-black night. Freezing cold stink, freezing cold claws. Milk-white wings beat cold-curdled air. Discreetly dry applause greeted the striking of my match.

The eagles were there.

To this day, I can only think they were automatons on display.

Scarcely had I time to protect my one remaining eye than they were upon me, gnawing at my hands. There must have been five, or perhaps seven of them. I thought I could see the grin and tie of a hanged man. Again, wings clapped my face. I would have jumped out of the tiny window, anything would have been better than this, but fortunately the roof looked out over an abandoned balcony and I trod on a cloud of shuddering doves feathers.

"Come," he said.

He was there, on the roof, squatting. From a distance, he had been watching out for me, but he didn't even glance in my direction.

"Come," he repeated.

"The Eagle," I said his name.

He smiled.

At lunchtime, harbour officials swarmed into the pizzeria as usual but, that day, a special table had to be laid for three detective sergeants. My uncle's body had been found and they were looking for me. The Eagle asked me to stay in the room full of shoes whilst they interrogated him. At about half past two, when the restaurant was closing, the doctor and his athletic friend arrived.

"This way, Mr Moretti," the Eagle showed him the way.

"Is it closed?"

"Not to you. Come on."

"I like to get straight down to business," said Moretti.

"We're ready," the Eagle answered. "All we need is your decision."

"Mine is already made," the doctor said.

"Alright? Who?"

"Wait and see."

"What about the rest of the crew?"

"That's all taken care of," the Eagle said.

"I'm sure it has been," said the doctor. "Mr Silver knows his business."

The Eagle reddened.

"Not so fast," he said.

He had the doctor by the scruff of the neck.

"Alright," said the doctor, "I've got the message."

"Good," said Silver.

He looked at me. He knew I would be calling him Silver too from now on.

Suddenly, he grew very polite.

"Do you want to eat?"

"Not yet. We'll hang on for a bit."

A sign from Silver told me I should make my entrance.

"This is the surprise I mentioned on the phone."

"It's no surprise. We've already examined him in hospital."

"Well?"

"He's too old."

"What do you mean, too old? What is that supposed to mean? He's still a child."

"If you insist."

Silver had gone white again. He was trembling.

"Are you surprised?" said Moretti.

"No, but..."

"Here he is," said the doctor. "We're ready now, we can order."

The boy entered. He moved slowly across the room. It was obvious his radiant footwear had won over Silver, heart and soul.

"Oh well," he said. "That's life."

"What's going on?"

Silver gave me a long, hard look and shook his head sadly.

"I regret to say that your application has been turned down."

The boy stared at me.

"Good afternoon, Captain," he said. And he gave me an exaggerated wink.

CHAPTER V

On the 4th September the birds invaded our ship of dreams between eleven a.m. and seven p.m., island time. The Captain's perpetual fear pre-dated this event by quite some time. He had, in fact, been nervous since the day Silver and our friends had brought their weaponry on board, something that had been specified in all the agreements. I have to say that the mechanisms leading up to inevitable conflict had never been so rusty; the crew were seized with a kind of nervous anxiety, a sense of vacuity and horrendous make-believe that was bound, in the end, to provoke the newspapers.

For suddenly our hastily cobbled together little expedition, never mind whether it turned out to be some kind of smokescreen or just a sort of nautical keep-fit exercise, was the centre of a great deal of attention. Let us just say that the smell of our unreliable ships' engines was not the only fishy thing about a trip which was characterized, more than anything, by a kind of languid fixation for the hulk we called our vessel, a fixation established by Moretti, the dilettante, and amply shared by banks of fog on our way.

The Captain was livid with rage. All the same, it's a miracle the boy did not have a trail of journalists traipsing after him. It was on everyone's lips. What was? I was absolutely convinced that nothing, nothing whatsoever, was premeditated in this carefully planned expedition.

That birds attract other birds is well known. A true colony of gulls and a multitude of sparrows followed us for days. Moreover, to the great delight of Silver, the ship's cook, a filthy cloud of parrots joined in.

Two days after our departure, I was put in charge of the boy. I didn't think I'd have any trouble talking to him about any subject of his choice; I didn't expect to have any problem playing with him, or singing to him. I was wrong. He turned out to be a born solitary. His only plaything was his body and his hands really were a sight. He always pretended not to listen when he was spoken to, or worse, to be deep in conversation with an imaginary person standing just behind you. These conversations of his were a deeply serious matter; they involved a great deal of hideous facial expression, such was the child's scheming innocence. He was an actor (this will come as no surprise to anyone familiar with the new rules of the game, now that auditions for the part are routine). He knew his lines and was well aware that the game he was playing had not even occurred to me.

I was about to give up when he took it upon himself to talk to me.

"My friend," he said. "It is a matter of some distress to me that, although I am, in effect, the pivotal point of this enterprise, I should nonetheless be expected to take part in entertaining digressions which are entirely improvised. I'm sure the Captain agrees with me."

He was obviously dying for an opportunity to stop pretending and go back to being a normal child.

"But it does seem slightly absurd to spend one's time spying on someone who is, in turn, spying on you."

Clearly, one of us was playing the wrong game.

"Look, son," I said, stupidly patronizing him, "don't you worry about the game I'm playing. You know perfectly well that I got myself into a spot of trouble. I'm only here because I'm in hiding."

"That same old story," he replied. "Did you know the diamond was real?"

"So what?"

"Well, it's a jolly serious matter, isn't it? I mean a diamond is worth an awful lot. That's how I got this job, after all."

"What job?"

"This job."

"I don't believe you."

"Why not? Money talks, doesn't it?"

"If you say so," I muttered.

"I do. Listen: I've still one diamond left. It's yours if you help me find the answer to a riddle that's been bothering me. It has nothing to do with this game which, incidentally, is just a job to me."

"What's your riddle?"

"Who is Midas?"

"I don't know."

"I didn't think you would. No one seems to know. Nevertheless I'm convinced you're the only person who can get near him."

"Why?"

"Because he messed up this job."

"Is he a child?"

"Oh no, he messed it up ages ago."

"What do you mean, ages ago?"

"My poor boy, I believe those idiots have really missed their chance. They've let the best ones go. You're the real thing, you are."

"The real what?"

"A true Jim Hawkins. Still, let's press on. For the moment, I want you to dive right in there, down where this famous Midas character hides. I can't sleep because of him."

"Where is he?"

"Where would he be if not here? His job is to report back everything I do. He's listening to us right now. Otherwise, how would he know what we're talking about?"

"I hope you don't mind me saying, I think you're a very cynical person."

"I'm glad to see you've some manners though. It would be inappropriate to get too informal, given that, in a few days' time, we're all going to be at each other's throats."

"You think?"

"I do and I don't. I'm a third generation Jim Hawkins. I'm perfectly aware of what awaits me."

"Oh, I see. What about me then?"

"I know, I know, it's always much harder for the random factor, isn't it? Still, if you do as I ask, I promise not to make you Israël Hands. Please say you will."

He had become a little boy again.

—

"Please help me. I'm scared."

"Let me think about it first."

"Think about what, for God's sake?"

And then Jim Hawkins burst into tears. So I did, in the end, agree to accomplish the most outrageous deed a man can be expected to perform. I agreed to spy upon myself.

But that is something that I was yet to discover. I set out to explore every nook and cranny of the ship. It was full of weapons and tropical fruit, full of birds of prey and rotting camouflage; but beyond all that, at the heart of the ship, there was a strange oasis, a place with a toy palm-tree and plastic camels. There was an office there too, a quite tiny place.

"I was expecting you," the voice said.

"And I was looking for you," I replied.

"I know what you've been up to, nothing escapes me."

"How?"

"I'm a professional."

He burst out laughing, dark and funereal.

"The same could hardly be said of you."

"I know."

"Oh really? You mean you're straight?"

"Not yet."

"That's good," he said.

A bullet grazed my left leg. I thought it was a good idea to break the light. In the dark, the birds recovered their breath. In a split second they swarmed into the oasis.

"Why did you do that?"

"Because I like my job. My time hasn't come yet. I'm still fit, I'm not prepared to go just like that."

"I have no desire to kill you."

"That's what they all say."

"I'm not lying."

I lit a paraffin lamp.

"Where are you?"

"Guess?"

I looked everywhere, but I didn't find him. I was cold and hungry. I ate an apple.

"It's obvious you've never read the book."

"I've skimmed through."

"You don't have to, you know. In fact, some people say it's better not to. But if you really haven't read it, how is it you didn't find me straightaway?"

I needed to think it through.

He emerged from the apple barrel. He looked pleased with himself.

"I should have been that Jim Hawkins really, but it's all so unfair. That's why I want to kill you. I could hardly do anything worse, could I?"

"I suppose not."

"Well, you're wrong. I can think of something much worse. Watch."

He shot himself in the head.

The birds flew everywhere in a panic, their squawking crowning the sound of the shot. I should have run away. Or screamed. Instead I took the apple from the dead man's hand. I ate it slowly as I entered the barrel head first and then I fell asleep in the dark to the sound of Midas' final words.

"Sometimes, I have succeeded in anticipating the episodes of the treasure hunt, predicting the reversal of such and such a digression, foreseeing a blind alley that might, from time to time, have confused players who were too keen. I have never made a mistake concerning the part a candidate could play in the story. I just needed him to open his mouth. Even the random factors, those characters who thought they weren't playing a part and imagined this too was a genuine adventure, became unwitting victims of my cruel clear-sightedness. I have never had to interrupt the prescribed course of events, acted out by the formal participants, to find a role for the random factor: all I had to do was devise a sequence as far as possible from their expected course of action and they were trapped, ensnared in the evil web of my intrigue. They could not escape; death was inevitable.

"Yes, I'm bad. All the people who have played this part have been bad. Only a week ago, I was informed of a decision that had, no doubt, been taken several months earlier. I was not to be expelled (an inconceivable outcome given the nature of this institution) and they did not have the courage to kill me. But they had to get rid of me somehow; my presence has become a burden. They opted for the standard method: they gouged out my eyes. I was left with no choice: unable to write, I had to play the blind man, which is not a part I want to play. Apart from anything else, there are already three blind men on the waiting list so my chances of taking part in the next Treasure Island cycle are fairly slim. I have therefore taken the only honourable course of action left to me. I have always been an exemplary employee of the Association for the Promotion of Adventure and African Veterans. I will remain so till the day I die. My successor may rest assured. He will find everything in order."

His voice grew inaudible. Even in my dreams. Silver eventually came and woke me up.

"Here's your dinner. I want ten pages by eight in the morning, that's the rule."

"How do you know I can write?"

"A little bird."

"An eagle, more like."

Silver chuckled.

"I suppose I have to tell you my life story now. We don't all end up like our friend here. It took me three whole years, the longest years of my life. It's worse than going to jail."

"This is jail."

"On the contrary. You must walk around. It is absolutely imperative you get to know us better than we know ourselves. Your job is to give us our lines and they must come as a surprise every time, they must come out of the blue. We must live in fear of what's to come. We must be afraid of you, more than we're afraid of Fate itself. You are our future."

"Can I have you all killed?"

"I wouldn't advise it. Look at poor Midas."

"I see."

"Are you scared?"

"Yes."

"And so you should. The more frightened you are, the more fun your digressions will be. And believe me, we need you. So far, it's been a real bore."

"Tell me what you want."

"Imagination, justice, belief. You have to make this island exist."

"Why? Is there a possibility it doesn't?"

"That's up to you."

"I'm sorry, I don't understand. Are you telling me the island doesn't exist?"

"Yes and no. In ten years, the prize has only ever been won twice. It has cost a good fifty lives."

"But you had a map."

"A book. Which is not the same thing at all. It really restricts the chances of winning."

"I see."

"Just remember: there's always a random factor to determine what we do. Of course, even if we're on the right track, there's always a good chance that, at the end of each episode, each digression, we get blown right off course. Literally."

"And who decided what I'd be doing?"

"We did. It was our go."

"What about next time?"

"I have a feeling there might not be a next time. But then I'm sure we'll win it this time."

"What?"

"The prize."

"Because of me?"

"I hope so."

"This is starting to interest me."

"About time," said Silver. "Hurry up, your food's getting cold."

"I thought you were going to tell me your life story."

"Some other time. There's an awful lot. Anyway, it's boring."

That night, I decided we'd have a really good mutiny, and I was going to be in command.

CHAPTER VI

I have made my decision. There is something odd about writing a story in the past tense even though it has yet to take place. I suppose, the present tense would be better, and easier. I had started by saying: Silver's men gather on board the ship in a cabin near the galley. The sea is visible. Birds circle overhead, above the ship, a sign that the location must be quite close. A boy makes his way towards us, crossing the deck without appearing to notice us, though he knows I must be there. He vanishes from sight. Almost immediately, we see him in the canteen. He's hungry. He discovers the apple-barrel. A scout signals to Silver's men. One of them says, unnaturally loud, in a kind of theatrical way: "Oh no, we can't. We can't kill him." To which another replies: "Oh yes we can." And so on.

Now the boy reacts. Within thirty seconds he finds it. (He finds it without assistance, a point in their favour.) Now, they are all there. They argue. They are excited. There will be a mutiny. They vote on it. There, that's it. Silver's motion is carried by a comfortable majority. One by one, they file out. The boy is slow off the mark (one point to us). He has fallen asleep, as predicted, though I know it's dangerous to predict small details. It might almost be described as a professional fault: there is only one chance in ten that he will do what is predicted. Too late, it is written and there is a witness, reading these pages as I write who will, in any case, have given me a black mark (I can hear him laughing; he knew what I was going to write. He laughs again, lights a cigarette and paces up and down).

The others wait for a signal before getting into position. They come forward. They seem nervous and unsure of themselves. They are worried that something is going to happen. Some of them believe the faster

Silver moves, the greater his chances of winning. But not every one shares that opinion. Is it not the case that twice in the past ill-prepared mutinies have been a disaster for the pirates and, indeed, for the pursuit as a whole? But this time, the timing seems right. The good guys are behaving in a grown up way: no panic, no violent reactions. They are scared, as they must be, because the mutiny is one of the three points in the game when players risk their lives. The boy is alone in thinking there is no danger, which is one of the elements in the pirates' favour. The boy teases the doctor for being afraid; he thinks the doctor is pretending. Which can only lead to the Captain losing his temper and the doctor in turn bursting into tears.

Such are the events I predict upon this autumnal evening.

I attend the next day's events in a critical capacity, as an observer. My prophecy turns out accurately: everything I had planned takes place before my very eyes. The precision and unselfconsciousness of the action is extremely moving. As soon as the doctor had had his breakdown, the boy came straight up to me and said: "Well done." He gave me something: a diamond which he had at least had the good grace to wrap in a black handkerchief, and upon which were inscribed in chalk the words "I resign." But this was going too far. He knew too much. Nothing is riskier than to try and subvert the natural order of procedure (I have to say that I predicted yesterday that I should write these lines today).

Two days passed, then I started to take myself too seriously. Something that I had also foreseen. But how on earth could I have written things as hard to concoct as the accident in the engine-room, the fall of Israël Hands or the good guys' resolution to abandon ship...

The fact is that I did and that these things were foretold three nights ago. I want everything I predict from now on to be just as surprising and equally inevitable.

Now, I write every day, I predict whole clusters of events and landscapes rich in detail that I invent myself; I foretell states of mind and parallel series of action that no one can verify. It doesn't matter, I have fallen into the trap and I am beginning to understand some of Midas' more enigmatic words.

The pirates celebrated their apparent victory at a great gathering, a heavy-drinking banquet. When the time came, I got to my feet and abandoned them to their fate. I had guessed, you see, what was bound to happen within the next ten minutes.

Considerable damage was done. Two men died and had to be disposed of in the boiler. And they have given up all hope of capturing the fugitives.

Certain members of the crew have discovered my clairvoyance and they consider me with a kind of cautious curiosity akin to the respect pious women show a priest. My witness has been changed four times. In theory, his function is to make sure that the writings are genuine and that I clock up the requisite number of working hours. My daily script is called a call-sheet. Every morning, each of the players receives a copy and, at the end of the day, we held a meeting to assess the day's work and outline the following day's programme.

But the players' attitude has altered profoundly since I've begun to describe their innermost feelings. At first, they protested (I had predicted this, of course) but in the long run their curiosity got the better of them.

My current method is that I start off by writing down a sequence of events without specifying the players' intentions or any kind of detailed action. This is called the plot. Then I go on to describe each of the characters' hidden motives, any last minute changes which may occur and the range of possible events arising from certain flaws in the game. The sum total of flaws in the game constitutes the final plot. Flaws actually determine the underlying force of events. As I see it, the course of events is a kind of fluid but unbelievably cumbersome, raw material out of which emerges an unexpected and inexplicable sequence: the actual story-line. The story is, therefore, in polarized opposition to the game.

Why then do we bother with the game at all? It is an exhausting and dangerous process.

I know, or rather, see, that the day will come when all the events of my life will crowd around me in a fanatical disorder. I shall make a speech in which each event will be referred to by its surname. Then we'll have a military parade in which the events will participate: my whole life on parade. The only problem with this is that I can see no end to my parade. It is infinite. I shall thus have to invent a game, a game with only one rule: each one of the events of my life will be required to select and identify with a specific word in my speech. Comfortably arranged in a vast and tranquil park, they will pronounce, by order of appearance in the speech, their word. By the end of the speech, my life will seem to me to be both fruitful and mercifully short.

The reason for this digression is that I have now been banned from making any sort of prediction. My role as narrator will, in short, only have lasted a few days. Long enough for me to have gone crazy about the future. In any case, one consequence is that no one else in the crew will speak to me. No one speaks to me, for no one wants to know the immediate future.

So what's the point in telling you my most recent vision? Last night, as I was sleeping, a recurring dream which had been growing more and more specific with every passing night suddenly came to me with blinding clarity. I saw the desert; it was there, in front of my very eyes. Then, in a paper-white sky, there appeared the following words: *the island is not in the sea. It is a long way from your destination*. Immediately, I saw a kind of abandoned fortress. And I heard the voice of the woman I love more than anything else in the world. She was calling me.

The next day, I decided to abandon ship. I planned my escape meticulously, down to the last detail. I acted calmly for I was confident of its success. As far as I was concerned, the adventure of Treasure Island was over and a real adventure was about to begin. When the time came, however, my plan failed for the most absurd reasons. I had determined that I should escape during one of our stopovers at a deserted island in the Treasure Island Archipelago. I must admit that I had formed the unfortunate habit of not looking right when I was foreseeing the future. Consequently, I had not noticed that there was a yacht to our right. Silver's men decided to board it.

The crew offered no resistance. Silver went on board with a man called Narvaes who, until now, had played only a minor part in the events I had been describing. I knew he couldn't stand the sight of me and, though my successor had chosen to give him some fairly standard things to do, including, I must say, two fairly decisive interventions, nonetheless he felt left out. In fact, he held me responsible for his abandonment. Poor man, the word *abandonment* killed him. One day, someone will peer into the bottomless pit of the Treasure Island archives. In that splendid marinade, it should be possible to find an explanation for all the accidents that reveal the power of words, and also possible to stroke the floating corpus that exposes the horror linked to a single word. *Visit*, for instance, is a word that has filled a thousand cemeteries, or what they call cemeteries, but which are in fact nothing more than endless stretches of sandy beaches inhabited by carnivorous crabs. As I was saying, I was not the inventor of those digressions, that day. I cannot therefore be held responsible for the unfortunate accident that led to Narvaes' death. Also, I should like to take this opportunity to thank the clerk who bore witness to the above in the document drawn up for our Lisbon office and which I now include in my personal memorabilia as evidence against the foul rumours clustered around my name. I must emphasize that, during the ten days I was there, I avoided making any reference, direct or indirect, to any type of explosive word.

Narvaes was brought back to the ship during siesta in order to spare those of us still capable of sleeping soundly the sight of his detached and dismembered limbs, an indubitably honourable display of bits which had suffered the impact of a booby-trapped device of a most appalling and unsportsmanlike nature. The poor man's eye-sockets had been covered in silver dollars; his atrocious head stuck out of an unrecognizable backside; his enormous belly spread beside a greenish arm whence a moralistic tattoo had prudently been removed, only to be transferred to his tongue which hung loose between a testicle and an ear; his ear in turn was stapled to a stray foot; his shoulder was dripping with excrement decorating his left thigh where also a multitude of nipples (more than two, I'm certain) had landed. None of which was in the slightest bit funny. In fact it shattered my plan for escape. What had happened?

Nothing serious, according to Silver. Just a slight misunderstanding. The man had had the misfortune to utter, just at the wrong moment, the word *abandonment*. Something which was apparently against the rules at the best of times and particularly offensive at that specific moment.

I really had lost track of our progress when I was asked to resign from my position as scribe but, apparently, we moved three stages with this episode, one death being worth three stages of the game. A decisive point had been reached but Narvaes had the last word.

The crew of the yacht came to dinner that very same night. Its captain, a Mexican officer with a big mouth, whose love of haughty amputation had got the better of his hatred of impure grafts, burst into graphic fits of laughter. He was endlessly rediscovering his peasant profile in mirrors and somehow it convinced him he was a true leader of men. During the three hours the meal lasted, he desperately tried to steer the conversation towards his favourite subject: *Benito Cereno*. A Treasure Island veteran (he had been party to four different sets of the game and, though his yacht was now out of bounds, he still took part as voluntary observer), he was always harping on about how much better that forbidden game was.

"I'm astonished to hear you say so," Silver exclaimed. "*Benito Cereno* isn't a game, it's just a pretext for gratuitous slaughter."

"In other words, not really slaughter at all."

"Murder by computer dating."

"Don't tell me you like *The Suicide Club*!"

"Well, if pushed, I'd rather choose *Time Regained*."

"And why not? A poof's a poof, I say. What about *Ulysses*, or *Aspern*, while you're about it?"

I was adrift upon the eternal lake of my single eye. Beneath the dome of a listening, though indifferent sky, our friends were moving rapidly towards my forecasts. They were, I saw, sinking into a kind of banal ferocity which they in no way deserved. And I was not, in point of fact, seeing, but reviewing the scene. As to the bullets on the brink, they were points of honour in a space dissected by two rivers that never met. I conceived the following metaphor: bullets perceived by my port-hole of an eye were points and this spattering of the sun, the extent of souls. The soul is equal to the body, such was the theorem I devised between two rounds of bullets. And the names of novels were tutelary ideas, each recognized figure plunged in an ocean of insults where it must discover the fish's sign so that death, or its essence, might begin the long journey upwards: traversing the four elements, or catholic virtues, crossing the five predictable principles; and overcoming the title to attain, at last, that exquisite place on high where future crimes shall reign at leisure. And in peace.

The fight resulted in three unnecessary deaths. Then, after negotiating for two hours, Silver and Mendoza signed an agreement and went off for a walk around the island. Someone woke me up just before dawn. We had, I was told, decided to go off on the yacht. Just like that. At noon, Silver called a meeting of all participants to announce that we would be including a chapter from a novel that, he said, he had long admired: *Benito Cereno*. Our job was to play the rebellious slaves while Mendoza would play the captain.

We spent the next three weeks circumnavigating the island in search of a suitable competitor. Twice we tried, and failed to board yachts. Morale was low but we were coping. We settled down to play cards.

Then one afternoon we all woke up simultaneously, right in the middle of our siesta. Some visions are true and our erections were there to prove it. They were all pointing in the same direction that was evidence enough. And once we closed our eyes, we shared the image of a woman, the same woman, appearing to every man. She led us a merry dance provoking the worst outburst of suspicion it has ever been my privilege to witness. She was our goddess. She had herself devised the immutable dance that catapulted us into a dream more naked.

We had been deceived. Silver had not told us the whole truth. She belonged neither to *Treasure Island* nor to *Benito Cereno*. She was *She*.

"Yes, she is *She*," yelled Israël Hand.

But Silver quickly realized he had nothing to gain by seeking to hide the truth from us. That night, we saw the incarnation of the dance. And it was her, the sister of the woman I love more than anything in the world.

She gave a speech of welcome. She was proud, she announced, to have been invited to join the game. She pretended to dance naked and vanished immediately, reappearing in a lunar guise, which was her natural form.

For several weeks more, we navigated. One stormy day, my prophecy materialized: the lifeboat of fugitives was there before us, a conjuring trick only tropical seas perform. They fell, literally, onto the deck of our yacht. They were all there, all four of them: the boy, the doctor, the squire and the captain.

Now we had to begin all over again. The game obviously had to be re-registered and Silver immediately ordered that a radio message should be sent to the office in Lisbon. The very next day, the action resumed.

If I am still alive today, it is only thanks to the imagination displayed by our tropical scribe. Mendoza had been nominated leader. Characteristically, he set about arranging at once for the multiple rape of the only woman on board. Silver was against it, but the rules demanded that he should consult the entire crew. And the crew had lived through too many novels without a single female character. Silver lost.

The rape began at about three in the afternoon. When my turn came, most of the men were asleep, scattered about the deck. Each man slept in a most ostentatious position, so that, as a group, the crew gave off a subtle aroma of voracity. They were the yellow wind that already played with the coming storm. Sailors' bodies had taken on the lively, naked form of birds excrement. They were all dead, though I did not yet know it, for the art of prophecy engenders scepticism. *She* was expecting me when I entered her cabin, but she was not naked.

"You'll just have to manage," she said, without any form of hate.

Israël Hand, Rolda and Mix lay exhausted in the corner.

"Do you mind being watched?"

"I'm not going to rape you," I said. "I'm a Catholic."

"That's novel!"

I thought I heard a derisive laugh that froze my blood.

"That must come as a relief to you?" I said.

"Oh, I'm over the moon!" she exclaimed. Her laughter turned insane.

"How many Catholics are there on board?"

"Only me."

"No, my friend, you're wrong."

"Really?" I said in surprise.

"Oh yes. They're all perfect gentlemen, they are," she assured me.

"I'm glad to hear it."

"The thing is, young man, I'm not like other women."

"You mean you want me to rape you, is that it?"

"I can't stand inconsistency. First they tell me I'm going to be raped, then nobody rapes me. And now, of course, it's too late."

"Too late for them."

"That's right. Too late for them. Here, drink this." She offered me a glass.

"No thanks, I'd rather stay alive."

"Brilliant!"

Someone was laughing somewhere in the cabin.

"Abandonment!"

Everything suddenly made sense. The forbidden word had been spoken. She must have killed them all.

"Strange," I remarked. "It smells of sex in here. What exactly have you been up to?"

"I raped the lot of them," she replied with a blush.

"You did!"

"No, not me. He did, he did it for me."

"Who did?"

"Him... well, this... "

She opened a cupboard. A vast pile of heaving tripe that stank of Eau de Cologne and aftershave stared me in the face.

"The enemy again," he said. "Don't be scared. I've forgiven you."

"I don't believe you," I said.

The woman emitted a piercing shriek. I swear I'd barely moved. All I did was put out his hellish eyes. I crushed the squishy squid-like thing that passed for a nose and cut his bifidated member with my Swiss knife.

As I left, I heard the woman say:

"I thought you were friends."

"We were," I replied. "A long time ago."

EPILOGUE I

The end of the expedition was a disaster. It did not put an end to the journey, for I was determined to see with my own eyes the events I had prophesized so clumsily. I will spare you the details. Suffice to say that it took up ten years of my life. It is the subject of a forthcoming volume of memoirs.

In the end, I did discover the island. It is not in the Treasure Island Archipelago at all, but in the middle of a desert. It is not an oasis, but the ruins of an eighteenth century fort. I did not find any treasure there, but then it did not occur to me to look. I spent the best ten years of my life in that desert with the woman I love more than anything else in the world.

I learnt to play the piano there.

Of course, I was much younger then, and mischievous.

It was a long time ago.

EPILOGUE II

My father wrote this book shortly before taking his own life by burning himself alive. I have decided to allow its publication in the hope that it will furnish irrefutable proof of his insanity to those who persist in denying his profoundly unbalanced mental condition. My father was a very sick man. He warmed to his own wounds as others warm themselves beside a fire. It is important to note that, on the occasion of his last visit to me in my cell here, as I reproached him for not allowing me to read his memoirs, he replied curtly that they were not his own memoirs but those of his father-in-law. He believed himself to be a living incarnation of his father-in-law, a celebrated anthropologist whose magnificent collection of coloured glass eyes is still in my possession.

I should also like to take this opportunity of acknowledging my gratitude to my father for setting fire to his tragic scars at last, and for taking the trouble to do so outside the walls of the prison I inhabit.

Arson is my passion. And he knew it.

printed by

DZS GRAFIK

Slovenia - EUROPE

August 2008